AMBUSHED

Presented to:
Stutsman County Library
In memory of
NELLIE COUNCILMAN

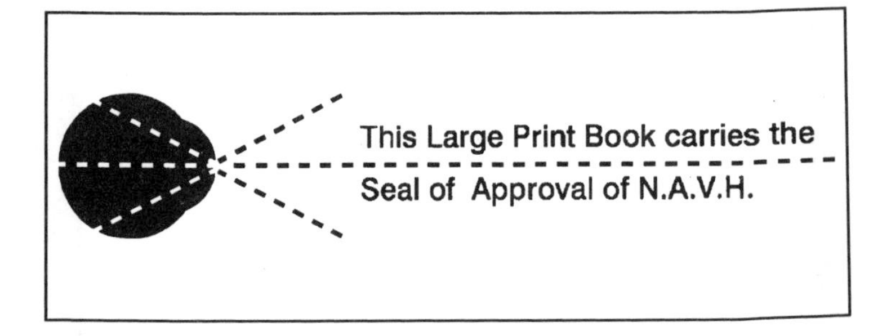
This Large Print Book carries the
Seal of Approval of N.A.V.H.

THE CONTINUED ADVENTURES OF
HAYDEN TILDEN

AMBUSHED

J. LEE BUTTS

WHEELER PUBLISHING
An imprint of Thomson Gale, a part of The Thomson Corporation

Detroit • New York • San Francisco • New Haven, Conn. • Waterville, Maine • London

THOMSON

GALE

This is a work of fiction. Names, characters, places, and incidents either are the product of the author's imagination or are used fictitiously, and any resemblance to actual persons, living or dead, business establishments, events, or locales is entirely coincidental.

Wheeler Publishing Large Print Western.
The text of this Large Print edition is unabridged.
Other aspects of the book may vary from the original edition.
Set in 16 pt. Plantin.

LIBRARY OF CONGRESS CATALOGING-IN-PUBLICATION DATA

Butts, J. Lee (Jimmy Lee)
Ambushed : the continued adventures of Hayden Tilden / by J. Lee Butts.
p. cm. — (Wheeler Publishing large print western)
ISBN-13: 978-1-59722-504-5 (softcover : alk. paper)
ISBN-10: 1-59722-504-5 (softcover : alk. paper)
1. United States marshals — Fiction. 2. Outlaws — Fiction. 3. Large type books. I. Title.
PS3602.U893A8 2007
813'.6—dc22 2007002379

Published in 2007 by arrangement with The Berkley Publishing Group, a member of Penguin Group (USA) Inc.

Printed in the United States of America on permanent paper
10 9 8 7 6 5 4 3 2 1

For Carol,
whose courage over the past year still
amazes me . . .

Samantha and Kim,
couldn't have done it without them . . .

and

Matt McKinley,
in the sure and certain belief that full
recovery is only a matter of time.

ACKNOWLEDGMENTS

Special thanks to my Internet group known affectionately as The Campfire. A list of their names would include some of the best writers of Westerns living today. Their knowledge and advice has proved invaluable over the years. When I can't find the answers anywhere else, they are an absolute fount of information and encouragement. And when it comes to the DFW Writer's Workshop, well, there just aren't enough words to express my gratitude.

"Think of yourself that every day is your last; the hour to which you do not look forward will come as a welcome surprise."

— Horace, *Epistles,* I, iv, 14.

". . . the death of a dear friend would go near to make a man look sad."

— *A Midsummer Night's Dream*
Act V, Scene 1, 295.

"In answer to a question as to what sort of death was best, a sudden death."

— Plutarch, *Lives,* Caesar
Sec. 32.

Prologue

Last night Chief Nurse Leona Wildbank tucked me into my bed, here at the Rolling Hills Home for the Aged, and said, "Don't let me come back in here and find you smoking one of those nasty cigars you favor, Hayden Tilden. Can't imagine anything worse than having you go to sleep and setting yourself on fire, old man."

Said, "For crying out loud, woman, you won't let me drink, ain't a warm female left alive that'll have anything to do with a man my age, and now I cain't even have a decent smoke? Being almost ninety years old sure as hell ain't turned out the unbridled fun it's cracked up to be — far as I'm concerned."

She finished snatchin' at my sheets, then headed for the door, but stopped on her way out, turned, and shook an accusatory finger at me. "You heard what I said. Either you behave, or I'll take those stinking stogies away from you altogether. Won't even let you smoke 'em on the sun porch."

Once she'd closed the door and got pretty well out of earshot, I said, "Get the hell out of my room, woman."

General Black Jack Pershing must've snuck in at some point in my disagreement with that mule-headed gal. He jumped up on my bed and curled his yellow-striped, fuzzy self on my stomach, and immediately went to sleep. I stroked the purring beast for a spell. Must've dozed off myself. Ghost of Captain H. J. Merchant wandered smack into the middle of my nightly dreams.

Last time I saw Henry Merchant amongst the living, we'd eaten a right pleasant lunch at the Pine Cone Café over on Rogers Avenue in Fort Smith. By then, both of us were retired from federal service, and I had taken up a town marshal's badge down in Texas. Everyone who mattered always agreed that when it came to Hanging Judge Isaac Parker's corps of dedicated deputies, Captain Merchant had no peer.

Over a steaming cup of freshly ground, first-rate, up-and-at-'em juice, we got each other apprised of the present pretty quick. Conversation drifted off into the past before I could stop it. Didn't take long for me to figure out that my old friend wasn't doing well with his newfound retired-lawdog leisure. Man was steeped in the long ago and the far away and, sadly, couldn't seem to tear himself out of it.

"You know," he said, in a voice raspy from tobacco smoke, "I was one of Judge Parker's men for more'n twenty year." Could tell from the wistful tone he pined for a return to the work.

Saluted him with my coffee cup and took a long sip. Then, I said, "Yes, Cap'n, I knew that."

He stared into the dark liquid sitting on the table in front of him, as though looking for something he might have missed. "Back during them bloody days, Hayden, I managed to maintain a hard-won reputation as a good man to ride beside in the Nations — dependable — stalwart."

"Never knew anyone to say otherwise, Cap'n. Everyone agreed you were a damned fine deputy U.S. marshal, trail mate, and one hell of a leader." The truth's the truth. No point in not acknowledging it when the opportunity comes along. Merchant was always one of the best. Didn't hurt me, even a little bit, to admit it.

He gifted me with a weak smile, then raised his own mug, as though offering a toast. "Nice of you to say so, Hayden. Coming from a man of your dedication, skill, and reputation, that means a lot to me."

"You know, Cap'n, the time you caught Martin Joshua might well develop into an oft-repeated legend before we're completely over and done with this life. Between his capture and the business with them snakes afterward, it's still one my favorite tales of your amazing exploits."

He cast a tired glance through the café's thick plate-glass window. Spent about five seconds examining the bustling street outside. "Yeah. Evil son of a bitch killed Bubba Stone, raped and murdered the boy's sixteen-year-old bride of ten days, and dumped both their poor broken bodies into a hell-deep crevice inside a cave up in the Arbuckle Mountains."

"Horrible damned shame," I said.

"Surely was. Poor kids had gone on their wedding trip at them waterfalls over that way. Took some serious detectin', but I finally ran ole Martin to ground in Muskogee. Cowardly bastard tried to hide under a pile of wet clothes in a Chinese laundry."

"Heard you beat him within an inch of his worthless life that day."

A halfhearted grin flitted across his thin, cracked lips. He rubbed at the stubble on an unshaven chin. "Tried my level best to kill the useless piece of human trash. Did all the damage I could with a pistol barrel. Whipped his ass like the gutless, slinkin' yellow dog he was."

"Every marshal in the Nations breathed a sigh of relief when word came around as how you'd caught him."

He picked at a ragged fingernail for a second, and looked lost. "Must have mislaid my temper for a few minutes when I wrapped my fingers around his scrawny neck. Guess maybe I shouldn't have let my personal feelings get the best of me the way I did. Trouble was, I knew those kids. Attended their nuptials with my wife. Both of 'em had a bright future and long, productive lives ahead."

I knew exactly how he felt. Vengeance is a hard thing to put aside, though. Could testify from personal experience that when the blood gets up, there are times when it's mighty hard to shove it down. Killing men gets to be right easy, when you've been at it long enough. Especially when you manage to catch one who's responsible for brutally murdering two fine young people you counted as friends.

"Wouldn't beat on myself too bad for whompin' upside ole Martin's head, Cap'n. Had it been my lot to take the man down, he would have come back to civilization wrapped in his saddle blanket, suitable for quick burial. Hell, me, Billy Bird, or Carlton J. Cecil would have shot him deader'n a fence post right where we caught him. Them Chinky fellers would've been rewashin' their laundry because of the blood he leaked on it."

My table partner poured himself another beaker of belly wash and stirred in a spoon of sugar. "Well, it's nice of you to say it. Damn, you know I still have nightmares 'bout them snakes, Hayden. Brought ole Martin in and the prosecuting attorney said, 'Merchant, we need the bones of Joshua's victims to make this case stick.' Hell, I was a lot younger then. Eyeball-deep in piss and vinegar, hopped up on my hind legs and said, 'I'll sure as hell get 'em for you, sir.' "

"Tell me, Cap'n, is it true that your partner, Spenser Taggert, volunteered to go down in the hole first?"

He actually chuckled at the memory. "Yeah. Me and Elwood Parker looped a rope around ole Spense. We musta played out about sixty feet of hemp lowerin' the bug-eyed boy into that pitch-black pit. He carried a kerosene lantern in one hand, a pistol in the other. Soon's the poor joker's feet hit the bottom of that stony cut, man went to hollerin', 'Christ Almighty, pull me up! Pull me up, now! Be quick about it, boys!' "

"Scared him some, huh?"

Merchant slapped the top of the table, threw his head back, and laughed out loud for the first and only instance. "We got Spenser back to the surface in record time. Man's eyes were as big as dinner plates. He ripped that rope from around his body and could barely talk. Stammered, 'Pit's full of the biggest damned rattlers I done ever seen, Cap. I sure as hell ain't a-goin' back down there.' Well, we had to have whatever was left of them skeletons. So I wrapped my arms, legs, and neck with some of the burlap bags we'd brought for the bones, and went down myself."

"It was a damned risky move, Cap'n. Only man I ever knew who survived a rattler's bite was Curtis No-Nose Bales. Sliced off his own beak with a bowie knife 'bout a second after the snake bit him. Poor son of a bitch bent down to pick up something shiny beside a fallen log next to a creek off the Wildhorse River. Big ole snake was hid under the log. Just never know, do we. Man looked right scary without a snout, but by God, he lived where most folks would have surly died a horrible death."

"Well, Taggert didn't miss the mark by much when he said that ugly chasm in the earth's hide was full of them deadly buggers. Worst of it was the beady-eyed rattlin' bastards had wadded themselves into, and around, those kids' bony remains like ribbons in a virgin's hair. So dark down there the lantern must'a blinded 'em some, leastways at first. Biggest one in the bunch struck at me, and missed. Blew his head completely off, just in nick of time. Thing still ended up coiled around my arm and neck — all seven feet of him. Shot two more of 'em to pieces as well."

"Gives me the willies just thinkin' 'bout it, Cap'n. God Almighty, I hate snakes."

"Worst of it was all that blastin', guess maybe it was the third or forth shot, concussion blew my light out. Them was the longest two minutes, or so, of my life. Thought I never was gonna get that lantern lit again. Was shakin' so bad, bet I broke half-a-dozen lucifers."

He stopped, looked thoughtful for a spell. Fiddled with his coffee cup some more. Kind of twirled it around in the saucer — two or three times. His chin quivered.

Mighty hard on the man when he finally said, "But you know, Tilden, I managed somehow to pick up all of it. Every bone, every shred of rotting clothing. Still had that big ole headless rattler wrapped around my arm and neck when I got back to the top. Poor Spenser almost passed out."

"Fine work, Cap'n. Mighty fine work."

"Yeah. And when Parker's prosecutor dumped those pitiful bags out on a table in front of the jury at Martin Joshua's trial, only thing you could hear for five minutes was people weeping."

"Didn't take those good folks long to render a verdict, from what I remember," I said.

"Twenty minutes. Judge sentenced the evil son of a bitch to hang. His departure from this world would've happened a lot damned quicker, too, but for the efforts of some mighty slick lawyers."

"Damned lawyers kept many a bad man at his chosen profession even after good people like us did the right thing. Whether they were horse thieves or murderers, some of 'em still managed to get off."

"Belly-slinkers kept that murderous skunk alive for almost a year, appealing the outcome of his day in court. But the end time finally came for him, in spite of all their slimy ways."

"Yes, indeed. I remember when his time came."

"I was out in the Nations. Heard as how the date had been finalized. Made a special trip back to Fort Smith. Couldn't really afford it, but I purchased me a ticket on the M.K. & T. just so I could bear witness to his departure. Got here just in time to see ole Maledon drop the Gates of Hell's twelve-man trap on the murderin' scum."

"Actually got to see Joshua swing, huh?"

"His sorry neck cracked like a rotten cottonwood limb. Watched him mess his pants, and then waited till they cut him down. Walked the corpse to the cemetery. Stayed till they'd covered him over. May well have been the most satisfying day of my entire career with Judge Parker."

"Always was a pleasure to observe a real bad man's sweet departure and subsequent meeting with Satan."

"No, Hayden. The real pleasure with Joshua came after the diggers left. Sat by his final resting place, took my time, and drank me a celebratory bottle of ten-year-old Scotch whiskey. Then, I pissed on his fresh-dug grave before going home to the pleasures afforded by my own dear wife and sweet children."

For the first time since we'd met that day, he got a satisfied, almost beatific, look on his face. We sipped at our cups, recalled more fond memories of friends we'd lost, men we'd killed, deeds — good and bad, and history long forgotten but by a few of us who still lived. I shook his once-powerful hand when we parted. Felt a deep sadness as I watched him amble away. Never saw Henry Merchant alive again, after that morning.

Heard from mutual friends, some years later, that good and decent man sat down at his kitchen table one cold winter night, put the barrel of a loaded .45 in his mouth, and blew the top of his head, and most of his brain, onto a spot over the cookstove. Deputy I know told me that all manner of skull bone and head-filler dripped down on the hot iron below and still sizzled, when he arrived to investigate. Said the room smelled like hog brains and scrambled eggs cooking.

Poor Merchant's wife was awakened by the shot and found him. Must have been mighty hard on the woman, and his boat-load of grown children. Damned sad end to such a fine fellow. Suppose he must have gone insane. That's the only reason I could come up with for an act of such obvious desperation. But who can know another man's heart — or mind? I often think of our chance meeting and the pleasant recollections of our fiery pasts.

Hell, I always come back to that meeting with Cap'n Merchant when I seek to justify my encounter with Maynard Dawson, Charlie Storms, and a host of others. Up till Charlie Storms, my *personal* vengeance had been relegated to the murderous Saginaw Bob Magruder. And even though I had Magruder dead to rights, and under the gun, I managed to hold off on killing the man. Brought ole Bob back to swing on Mr. Maledon's Gates of Hell gallows. So I completely understood Merchant's pleasure at watching a heartless killer shit his pants for a crowd of onlookers that usually numbered in the thousands. Thought it the right thing to do, at the time, and still do.

But with Charlie Storms, my God, even Satan couldn't possibly have figured out a worse death than I got in mind for that murderous villian before our final bloody dance eventually played out. Storms was one of the worst of the worst. A hell-bred murderer of men, women, and children from the day his momma pushed him into an unsuspecting world.

But the gruesome fact that he personally ended the lives of at least a dozen people wasn't the most horrible part of his story. Oh, hell, no. It was the way he did it, my friends. The hideous, blood-chilling way he went about his heartless killings. Never saw anything like it before, or since. And neither had anyone else I knew at the time.

What that man did to a human body makes the blood run cold, even on hot summer afternoons like this one today. Still gives me chicken flesh when I think about finding the broken, abused corpses he left behind. Reminds me, in no uncertain terms, that for more years than I'd like to admit, my life's calling was that of a special, secretly appointed assassin paid to kill men like Maynard Dawson, Charlie Storms, and Cotton Rix without mercy.

And, you know, deep down I genuinely enjoyed the work. Gave me no end of satisfaction to snuff the lamp on men responsible for such wickedness. The hair might stand up on my arms when I think about all those bastards and the crimes they heartlessly committed. But, at the same time, a smile of gloriously righteous satisfaction still spreads over my face when I remember the last light of life passing from their eyes when I put a bullet in their brains.

To my eternal dismay, many God-fearing men would self-righteously condemn me for such feelings. Same fellows would virtuously opine that as soon as good folk decide to use any means necessary to fight iniquitous behavior, their most worthy actions quickly become unrecognizable from the villainy they seek to destroy. The people who believe such bilge are idiots. And, yes, by God, I still smile each and every time I think about killing the hell out of Charlie Storms.

1
". . . Kill Maynard Dawson on Sight."

One of the first things Hanging Judge Isaac C. Parker did upon his ascension to the bench for the Western District Court of Arkansas, which included the bandit- and killer-riddled Indian Nations, was hire two hundred deputy U.S. marshals. After he swore all the new recruits, the judge admonished us to "Bring them in — alive or dead."

Sixty-five of those marshals gave their lives fighting bad men in the service of that admonition. On a number of occasions, as many as four and six at a time went down when waylayed by those who weren't fit to shine those brave law-bringers' boots. Such blood-soaked events followed, one upon another, for the whole twenty-one years Judge Parker held sway over the most lawless region this nation ever had to deal with.

Once heard the judge speak at a church gathering right after a number of his good men died in an ambush. Think he must have awakened in a contemplative mood that morning. During a rambling talk that lapsed into the philosophical, he kind of offhandedly said, "Isn't it strange how life is very much like a chain, and each event that occurs forms a link that binds us to the future. How one incident seems to lead, inexorably, to the next."

For some years after that morning's talk, I often contemplated what he'd said. Upon considerable reflection, I came to believe my own experience might well be the perfect example of what he'd described.

Life as a Kentucky farm boy ended for me when Pa decided to move to Texas so we could live near his brother. That decision led to my family's utter destruction at the hands of the murderous Magruder gang along the Mississippi in Arkansas. Thence to employment as a deputy marshal by Judge Parker, and my secret arrangement with that grand adjudicator as the man he sent to deal the final fateful blow to those considered beyond the law's ultimate punishment.

Even my meeting of Elizabeth, and eventual marriage, never would have occurred had it not been for my arrival in Fort Smith. Each and every episode coupled to the last. The progression of life has always seemed interconnected — how else can you explain God's great plan? Had it not been for the judge, I'd never have realized any of it.

One of the worst links in the chain of my life involved a lethal son of a bitch named Charlie Storms. My nightmarish experience with the man actually started when that red-haired demon with a pistol, Deputy U.S. Marshal Carlton J. Cecil, my friend Deputy Marshal Billy Bird, and me were out in the Nations trying to run Maynard Dawson to ground. Those friends and I formed the core of a secret group of man-killers we named the Brotherhood of Blood. When all else failed, the Brotherhood went out and brought them down. We always left them dead, dead, extremely dead.

Maynard Dawson was a six-and-a-half-foot-tall, one-eyed humpback with a mean streak as wide as the Mississippi River. Evil brute had a record of lawless behavior that ranged from stealing out of the plate at church services as a three-year-old child, to raping his own twelve-year-old sister a few days after he turned fourteen. He'd been in jail more times than a sixty-year-old soiled dove, from Hell's Half Acre in Fort Worth, has been fined for practicing her chosen profession. But the act that set the Brotherhood on his trail took the proverbial cake.

Carlton, Billy, and me went out looking to kill Dawson after he broke into the home of a rancher named Tom Black. Black ran horses on a nice piece of grassy bottomland a bit south of the Canadian River, not far from the old Chisholm Trail in the Chickasaw Nation. Hear tell he made a right fine living selling and trading with the passing herds on their way north to the Kansas railheads.

Dawson kicked Black's door down during a thunderous rainstorm punctuated by pitchfork lightning. Caught the rancher by surprise and unarmed. Shot the poor man dead, right in front of his wife and two young children. Then he attacked the wife while the kids looked on in horror. Soon as he'd finished with the unfortunate woman, the pitiless monster went after Black's thirteen-year-old-daughter.

We knew all this because while he performed unspeakable acts on that poor young girl, her distraught brother escaped the insanity, ran four miles, and reported the whole incident to a stunned neighbor. Only thing the boy couldn't testify about involved the unutterable way his mother and sister died. I'll not describe their passing here. Suffice it to say, trail-hardened marshals who investigated the murders wept when they discovered the brutalized bodies.

Two weeks after the slaughter, George Wilton, Judge Parker's chief bailiff, sent for me. When his note came, I knew my special talents, and perhaps those of the Brotherhood, were about to be put in play and that someone would die as a result — maybe more than one.

He guided me to the chair in his office I'd become very much accustomed to and, in his beautifully fluid Southern accent, said, "Please sit, Marshal Tilden. As you've probably surmised, Judge Parker has an assignment for you."

Squirmed around and made myself comfortable. "Always happy to serve in whatever way I can, Mr. Wilton."

He took the chair behind his desk, and pushed a thick sheaf of papers across the highly polished mahogany top. "This file will apprise you of the details of the criminal activities of one Maynard Gaston Dawson."

"I've heard of the man. Most recently in connection with a triple murder and brutal double rape. Doubt there's much in here that can top such heinous activities."

Wilton's ebony face sagged. He rubbed at a heavily knitted, rapidly graying brow. And, for the first time since we'd met, the man looked like the weight of the world rested on his shoulders. After some seconds of contemplation, he said, "I wouldn't be too sure of that, Hayden. The man is a lifelong felonious criminal. Hardly a week of his entire time on this earth has not seen a deed most good people would deem worthy of the noose."

I couldn't let that one pass. "Well, how's he managed to stay alive and runnin' free to commit such acts for so long?"

My secret tie to Judge Parker sighed, threw his head back, and stared at the ceiling. "Luck, and lenient juries, I suppose, serve to explain such oversight. The man should have been hanged, or killed outright, more than twenty years ago. A goodly number of fine folk would still be alive had either of those happy occurrences taken place. And, given the nature of his crimes, I have no doubt the faithful have hit their knees on numerous occasions and prayed fervently for a man like you to deliver them from the unspeakable evil of his presence on earth."

I shuffled through Wilton's carefully arranged stack of wanted posters, arrest warrants, depositions, testimonials, statements, death certificates, jail records, and other highly official-looking papers. Glanced at each mournful document briefly before saying, "Judge Parker would prefer I not bring this man in for trial, I take it."

He didn't hesitate with an answer. "You take it right, sir. To make your instructions as clear as a pitcher of ice-cold springwater, you are hereby instructed to kill Maynard Dawson on sight. The sacred heavenly clock that ticks off his time on this earth has stopped. He just doesn't know it yet, or that you are the deadly instrument of his departure from the living."

"Am I correct in surmising that Sam Sixkiller and the men of his Union Agency police force haven't had any luck catching up with Dawson?"

"Yes, well, Captain Sixkiller and his fine band of men have their hands full at the moment with matters pursuant to criminal activity done by members of the Five Civilized Tribes. As the killer in question and all his victims, except Mr. Black's wife, were white, Judge Parker deemed it our responsibility to take care of the matter. As a courtesy, we have informed Captain Sixkiller of his decision by telegraph. Your way has been completely cleared for this undertaking."

"I'll probably need some assistance."

He waved his agreement. "Take anyone you'd like. I would imagine that Deputies

Cecil and Bird will jump at the chance to assist. As the three of you are well known and much feared in the Nations, I would suspect they are by far you best choices."

"I'll see to it, sir."

With that, he stood and extended a hand. "Judge Parker has complete faith that his wishes in this matter will be fulfilled at your earliest convenience, Marshal Tilden. Godspeed and good luck in your sacred mission."

Knew the conversation had come to an end. Headed down the hall to the U.S. marshal's office in search of my friends. Ran into Carlton soon as I stepped across the threshold. Little redheaded peckerwood was in rare form. He had a number of weapons, rags, and various types of cleaning equipment scattered around on a table we used in the marshal's vestibule.

"What are you doin' here, Carl? Figured you'd most likely be at home with the lovely Judith. Maybe doin' a little sparkin' between trips to the Nations."

He screwed around in his straight-backed, cane-bottomed chair, held a .45 Colt's frame and barrel assembly in his hand, and snapped, "Well, you'd be wrong. Woman done went and run me out of the house."

"Why?"

He dropped the pistol parts on the table, snatched his hat off, and ran oily fingers through sweaty hair. "She's mad at me, again."

"Again?"

"Hell, yes, Hayden. Been my experience ever since the day we got hitched that the female of the species tends to stay angry about something as much as eight days out of every ten."

Tried to sound reasonable when I asked, "What did you do, Carl?"

He stuffed his hat back on and threw me a withering glance. "Just what in hell makes you think I went and done something?"

"Well, Marshal Cecil, it's been *my experience* that women seldom get upset with their husbands over nothing. Most times, us hairy-legged types manage to unthinkingly cross over one of the numberless invisible societal or personally held lines they use to gauge our worthiness as men."

My friend pulled his hat down over his eyes and, though muffled by the battered felt head cover, I heard him mumble, "Oh, sweet Jesus, invisible lines, for Christ's sake." He sounded like a man who'd just been told by the Angel at Heaven's golden gate that he wouldn't be entering anytime soon.

"Come on, Carl, spit it out. You'll feel better once you've confessed and unburdened your soul."

He threw his hat on the floor, got all red in the face. "Sometimes you sound just like a Baptist preacher, Tilden. Christ on a crutch, if I'd of knowed a man has to stop being a man once he gets married up, I might not have chosen to do the deed."

"Still haven't answered the question, Carl."

"Well, dammit all, I stopped over at Hattie Ringer's place last night and had a few beakers of panther sweat with my old friend Sheriff Tater Johnson. Tater was only gonna be in town a few hours. He was passin' through Fort Smith on his way to St. Louis. Had a prisoner in tow. Hadn't seen him since he left here more'n five year ago. We had a damned fine sit-down-and-palaver session. Lasted till a few minutes after midnight. That's it. Swear 'fore Jesus, nothing else happened."

"How many minutes after midnight, Carl?"

"Aw, hell, forty-five or fifty."

I couldn't help but chuckle at his excuse-making. "So, it was after one o'clock in the morning when you managed to drag your seriously lubricated self home?"

His head dropped and he acted like a ten-year-old caught in the act of doing something nasty. “One-fifteen or so, I suppose.”

“Went home drunk, huh?”

“I did not. Like I said, only had a dram or two.”

“Dram or two?”

“Well, maybe three or four. But I was not drunk. I think well lubricated is a good way to phrase it. Happy, friendly, jocular, looking for some fun once I got home. You know what I mean — a little of the old slap and tickle. Felt like maybe we could chase each other around the bed a time or two. But, swear to Jesus, I was not drunk.”

“Jocular? Where on earth did you pick up a three-dollar word like jocular, Carl?”

He glanced up at me and snickered. “Well if you must know, I’ve heard Judge Parker use it in court. He’s real fond of rapping that gavel of his when folks laugh during a trial and snapping, ‘This jocular behavior will not be tolerated in my court! Any further jocularity and I’ll have the room cleared.’ ” He smiled, snatched his hat off the floor. “Good word, jocular. I like the sound of it.”

Have to admit he managed to bring a smile to my face. “Trust me, Carl. She’ll get over her mad spell. Things are gonna work out just fine."

"Yeah, well, they's days when I look to God and beg him to tell me why he let me see her nekkid out there in the Nations, two year ago. That's what done it, you know. She was takin' a bath when me and Billy was draggin' that cannon up to Red Rock Canyon to blow Martin Luther Big Eagle out of his hideout. Think her glisten' wet body went and made me crazier'n a sun-struck, yeller-bellied lizard."

"When it comes to certain women, Carl, we're all crazy as hell whether we've seen 'em nekkid or not. Ain't no vaccination against it either. Just being around the right one has the power to turn us into blatherin' idiots."

"Maybe you're right. Guess I should sneak back home and try to make it up to her somehow. Maybe I'll take her a sack of lemon drops. Gal has a serious sweet tooth. She really likes lemon drops."

"Well, get it done. Judge Parker just handed me a job, and I'll feel a lot better about the whole doo-dah if all the members of the Brotherhood are along for the ride. Need everyone to be sharper than a stropped razor."

My news perked him up, and the discussion suddenly got serious. "Which evil son of a bitch are we goin' after this time, Hayden?"

"Maynard Dawson."

A look of pain quickly rippled across his face and just as quickly disappeared. "Oh, Jesus, he's a bad 'un. 'Bout as bad as any we've ever took down, and he won't come along easy. Killed a boatload of men and won't give a single second's thought to rubbing us out as well."

Leaned over and whispered, "We're not bringing him back, Carl. There is no dead-or-alive choice here. His fate is already sealed."

He stood, looked me in the eye, squinted, and whispered back, "Damned good deal, as far as I'm concerned. Are you still paying the freight on our missions as the Brotherhood?"

"Absolutely. You get the going rate just like we'd brought him in for trial and suitable hanging. Mileage, warrants-served pay, any rewards, and all other monetary compensation is yours and Billy's to split."

"Damned fine to hear it, Hayden. We'll sure as hell need Billy along with us. I'll go find him. Know he'll be happy to get out again. Man ain't had a decent payday in six months. Hear tell he's been borrowing against his pay from one of them speculatin' bastards."

"Outfit some mules for the trip, too. I'll meet you boys at the ferry landing tomorrow morning."

"What time you wanna shove off?"

"No rush. Make it around eight. You and Billy should have breakfast with your wives, or loved ones, before we leave. I want to spend a quiet morning with Elizabeth; then we'll hit the trail."

"Sounds good to me, Hayden. We'll be there. Is Old Bear goin' with us?"

"No. My semi-Indian cohort took off two weeks ago for a visit with some of the Comanche folks he lived with back when they killed his family and stole him away as a child. You know how he is. Might well just appear out of nowhere. Thing that irritates me most is he took my dog with him. Caesar would come in mighty helpful right now, but he's gone, too."

"Yeah, too bad. Might could use some of Old Bear's knife work this time. Never can tell what kind of bloody situation might present itself."

As I headed for the door, my friend busied himself with reconstructing all his various instruments of destruction. Carl was meticulous about firearms. Man could lay down a wall of pistol fire of such intensity that it tended to frighten the hell out of the opposition, even if he didn't hit anything. I'd witnessed his and Billy's skill with firearms many times in the past and trusted both of them with my life.

Knew beyond any doubt that by the time we met at the Arkansas, the next morning, Carl and Billy Bird would both be packing so much iron their poor horses could barely stand. And that between the two of them, they would guarantee Maynard Dawson was nothing more than a walking corpse just waiting for us to show up so we could bury him. A smoldering, *pestulous* hell awaited that murdering skunk. And the Brotherhood of Blood was just the company of men to send him along the path that would have him shaking hands with Satan's imps at the earliest possible convenience.

2
". . . Nailed Someone Up Like Crucified Jesus."

Next morning I kissed Elizabeth, waved good-bye, and headed for the ferry crossing. Billy and Carlton arrived ahead of me, had thrown several large pieces of bedding on the ground for a place to lounge about, and were engaged in a heated discussion involving their various female problems.

"Ain't no way to understand a woman," Carlton snorted as I reined up beside them.

Billy worked paper and tobacco into a smoke, poked it into his mouth, and said between clenched lips, "That's the damned truth. You know, when we got back from chasing the Crook brothers all over hell and gone, I thought Lucy Waggoner was the one for me. Then, be damned if that loose-legged woman didn't up and run off with a cross-eyed, three-fingered whiskey drummer from St. Jo."

Carlton and me had not heard one thing about Miss Lucy's recent departure. As I stepped down from Gunpowder, Carlton grumped, "The hell you say? She ran off with a whiskey drummer?"

Billy scratched a lucifer on the leg of his canvas pants and put fire to his roughly rolled cigarette. "Hell, I do say. He was one ugly son of a bitch, too. Can't even imagine what Lucy saw in the woman-stealin' bastard. Worst part of the whole affair is that she evidently abandoned the poor gomer in St. Jo the day after they arrived. Rumor goin' round now says she hotfooted it to Kansas City, and is sellin' herself to the highest bidder down on Wyoming Street."

I'd heard such stories before. One of my wife Elizabeth's best friends had fallen in much the same manner. Tried to comfort my obviously agitated friend when I said, "There's always another woman, Billy. You'll find someone. She's just waitin' for you to show up. Could be the perfect gal is out there in the Nations right now and she'll seek you out on this very trip."

He looked at me like I'd grown another nose right in the middle of my face. "Mighty unlikely, Hayden." His head dropped and I couldn't see his eyes when he mumbled, "You know, I really thought Lucy cared for me."

Carlton grabbed our downcast friend

under the arms and jerked him to his feet. He brushed ashes off the front of the lanky boy's shirt. "Ferget 'er, Billy my boy. Let's go kill some bad men. Make you feel a whole lot better to put holes in Maynard Dawson. Git them big Schofield pistols of yours working and I'd bet you'll perk up, right smart. For certain sure, you'll forget that two-timin' gal soon as you blast the hell out of somebody evil."

Billy grinned like a schoolboy just thinking about such a happy eventuality. Life tended toward the hard and lonely back in them days, and I couldn't blame him for being upset. But he handled the situation as well as could be expected. Pushed those big pistols' butts forward with the palms of his hands and said, "Let's go git 'em." Less than an hour later, we'd crossed the Arkansas and were headed south into the land of criminal darkness and wicked uncertainty.

Took us almost three weeks of talking to anyone who'd stop long enough to get a handle on the direction Maynard Dawson set out on after he'd brutally murdered Tom Black and most of his poor benighted family. Actually surprised me that the information came our way as quickly as it did.

Iniquitous sorts blanketed the Nations and maintained a series of signal fires on hills and mountains in every direction. Killers and thugs always knew where lawmen were, almost without fail. Average citizen out in the wild places was, for very good reason, terrified of being seen in the company of Parker's men. Reprisals tended to be the norm for those who couldn't count on any established law enforcement within fifty miles of their ranch, store, farm, or residence.

Then, late on a cloudy afternoon of the third week, we happened on a feller Carlton knew who was fishing from the brushy bank of a rock-littered creek, just off the Canadian, a few miles from Tom Black's ranch. Poor man appeared some troubled by our appearance. But once Carl stepped down and talked with him for a few minutes, his skittish behavior abated a mite.

Carl eventually invited me and Billy over to join in on the discussion. "Hayden this here is Silas White Bird — Choctaw friend of mine. Silas lives not far from here, over in the Washita Valley. Former member of the Choctaw Light Horse. Educated in missionary schools. He might have some good news for us."

White Bird shook hands all around, and we gifted the man with tobacco. Billy lit him up once he got a fine-looking pipe loaded.

Edgy feller had relaxed considerable, by then, and got right talkative. He took a puff or two and used the pipe stem to point north and west.

"Seen Dawson and some others headed toward Chickasha two, maybe three days ago."

"How many others?" I asked.

"Oh, four or five. Maybe six. Hard to tell. They was movin' through them trees yonder on the far creek bank. Caught glimpses as they passed. Hid myself soon's I seen 'em. Them's the kind of men reasonable folk don't want no truck with. Dangerous to your health and general welfare. Killers, every one of 'em."

Billy chimed in with, "Did you know any of the men traveling with Dawson?"

"Couple. One looked like Cotton Rix. Mo Coyle and Mica Crow Dog ridin' with him, too. Can't say on the others. Couldn't see that well."

Carl slapped the leg of stovepipe chaps with his riding quirt. "Damnation, boys, I know that one. Cotton Rix is worth three thousand dollars from the M.K. & T. He's robbed them poor railroaders near half-a-dozen times over the years. Kilt several express men in the process. We catch ole Cotton and that's a thousand each."

Billy eyeballed Carl and scratched his stubble-covered chin. "Well, Mo Coyle ain't no slouch. Bank of Vinita posted him more'n a year ago. Last one I seen said he was worth fifteen hundred for his part in a robbery that resulted in the bank manager gettin' rudely shot to pieces for failure to open the safe fast enough."

"If Mo Coyle and Mica Crow Dog are part of this crew, then you can just about bet the Crowder brothers, Harvey and Buck, are somewhere nearby," I said.

Carl pulled a faded bandanna and wiped sweat from a dripping forehead and brow. "Best check all our weapons and make damned sure every smoke pole we're carrying is ready for action, Hayden. If what Silas says is right, and them others are along for the ride, this might well be the worst gang of killers in a single group we've seen in years. They could easily rank right up there with Saginaw Bob Magruder and his bunch, or even rival the Crook brothers when they was at their worst."

Billy pointed upstream a ways. "Why don't we pitch camp under that big cottonwood? Make sure everything's cleaned and loaded for action. Have a hearty meal and get a good night's rest atop this fluffy stand of grass. Wanna be sharp for whatever comes our way tomorrow."

White Bird left us a mess of perch and hotfooted it with no words of farewell soon as he got a chance. Not much talk, joshing, or run-of-the-mill leg-pulling that afternoon, or night. My companions and I turned our attention to the deadly necessities we deemed would help keep us alive when Dawson and his lethal crew fell under our guns. Billy couldn't have been more right about the situation. We needed to keep ourselves as sharp as the business end of Mexican hornets. Everyone crawled into a bedroll soon as it got dark.

Come morning, we had to ride more than a mile downstream before we could cross over and head back north. Picked up the trail exactly where Silas White Bird said it would be. Hadn't followed the track but about three hours when we reined up on a grass-covered hill that overlooked a ranch building surrounded by several split-rail corrals.

Billy leaned on his saddle pommel and said, "Feller that built this house must have had some military in his past. Looks like a fort. Bet you couldn't blast your way in with a six-pound Napoleon."

Carl pulled a long glass out, fitted it against an unblinking eye, and stood in his stirrups. He swept the area, then handed the collapsible scope to me. "Best take a good look down there, Hayden. Think them's bodies I see."

Spotted what he'd noticed immediately. "I count one just outside the door on the porch, and one over by the water trough. Sweet Merciful Father, Carl. What do you make of the barn door?"

"Looks to me like them evil bastards nailed someone up like crucified Jesus."

Billy threw both of us a fleeting glance, grabbed Carl's spyglass, and fixed it to his eye. "You boys are kiddin', right? Oh, no. I'll just be damned. Cain't be true. Looks like a woman to me, boys." He lowered the glass and slowly handed it back.

We hobbled our animals and left them on the treeless hill. Carefully picked our way down to a bloody scene of rampant, muderous insanity. It's a skin-prickling, eerie feeling no matter how many times you confront hideous murders done in such a brutal manner.

All of us dodged over to the poor woman nailed to the barn door first. Quickly discovered there was no need to hurry. She'd been dead for some time.

Billy shook his head and looked ill. "Ain't seen nothin' to match this since we found that soiled dove everyone called Sweet Sweet Sally what got nailed to the outhouse door behind Gopher Stanley's dance hall over in Muskogee."

Carl covered his eyes with a shaking hand. "Never caught whoever did that 'un either. Tell you the God's truth, boys, looks like the work of the same animal to me. Way too many similarities here. Even down to the placement of her feet." He glanced at the much-abused corpse for a few more seconds and stomped away. As he passed me, he mumbled, "Christ Almighty, how do men this sick get born and set loose on the world?"

We turned our attention to the rest of the shocking sight as soon as we got that unfortunate woman down and properly covered. Altogether, we found five bodies — two outside the house, two inside, and the woman. Lucky fellers outside had been shot, while those in the house appeared to have been hacked to death with an ax. All of them were sock-footed.

Carl growled, "Sorry bastards stole their boots."

Most experienced at tracking, Billy stood on the porch and pointed back to our mounts. "We had the right trail. The entire party came from yonder direction. Seven of

’em. Guess there’s one we didn’t account for. Sure would like to know who he is. They rode up in the yard. This poor fool musta come out to see what the party of strangers wanted. Think they climbed down, walked up to the step bold as brass, shot him right off, then stormed the house. Saved the woman for all the real fun. Did the job on her last. She must have been an Indian gal. Otherwise, this well-dressed white feller wouldn’t be livin’ out here.”

I said, “You’re probably right, Billy. She was burned so bad, I couldn’t have testified to her race. Guess we should take a second look just to make sure.”

Carl figured the corpse hanging half on and half off the front porch for the ranch’s owner. Dead man was a tall, healthy-looking gent, who’d been shot between the eyes with a big-bore weapon of some kind. A washbasin-sized gob of brain matter and bone decorated the front door in a splatter of dried blood and gore.

Carl knelt beside the body, snatched his hat off, and shook his head. “I’ve seen more’n my share of wounds like this before. Most likely done with a Sharps. Bullet went clean through the poor goober’s skull. Bet I can find it in the wall, or door, somewheres. Rest of these boys got shot, hacked, stabbed, and beat slap to death real quick soon as this poor trusting soul fell here by the door. House reeks of blood and murder. Got that coppery taste in my mouth when I was in there. So strong I cain't spit it up."

I toed the body in the doorway. "Looks to me like the entire massacre could have been avoided if this feller had stayed inside and kept the door barred. Can't imagine why he opened up and stepped out here when there was a bunch as disreputable-looking as Dawson's showed up in his yard. Hell's fire, don't even appear to me he was armed when he went down. Incredibly stupid, if you ask me."

Billy swept the entire scene into the conversation with the motion of one arm. "When do you think it all happened, Carl? Yesterday, or the day before? According to Silas White Bird, the Dawson bunch is at least three days ahead of us. What we've got here might just be the beginning. Depraved sons of bitches could have killed triple this many, by now."

"Well, these folks are startin' to ripen up pretty quick. Poor souls went down shortly after Silas seen Dawson's gang pass him back yonder on the creek. I'm thinkin' this unfortunate lot has been dead two days, at least."

Took some backbreaking, odoriferous lifting, and more time than we had at hand, but we got holes dug. Buried those folks before we left. Prayed over them some. Carlton fished a Bible out of the wreckage. Discovered the family was most likely named Wilson. He opened the book and surprised me by reading a passage from the Scripture. Thought he would ask me to read Shakespeare, but he must have figured God's word worked better than the Bard's.

"Whatsoever things are true, whatsoever things are honest, whatsoever things are just, whatsoever things are pure, whatsoever things are lovely, whatsoever things are of good report; if there be any virtue, and if there be any praise, think on these things. By Him were all things created, that are in heaven and that are in earth, visible and invisible . . . all things created by Him and for Him: And He is before all things, and by Him all things consist. The day of the Lord so cometh as a thief in the night. Amen." When he finished, Carlton dropped the book in one of the open graves before we covered them over.

The killers had taken an extra horse apiece from the dead rancher's corrals. We turned out all those left behind. Couldn't take them with us. Figured if we left them, the poor neglected beasts would have suffered for no good reason.

Billy didn't have any trouble putting us back on Dawson's trail. As we rode away from that unspeakable scene of carnage, Carlton pulled up beside me and said, "We had enough problems when it was just Dawson who had to be found. Got a creeping feeling of black doom about this, Hayden. Have a grinding suspicion this gang of yahoos are gonna turn out worse than the Crook brothers ever thought about being. Worst of it is, there's more of 'em."

"Could be, Carl. All we can do is catch up with 'em. Kill as many as possible. Blind justice might not be well served by what I've got planned. But once we've plugged 'em each, a time or three, they won't ever do anything as gruesome and cruel as this again."

3
"All Cut Open, Chopped Up, and Gutted Like That."

Perhaps the most interesting thing about riding for Judge Parker was always the unpredictability of the work. Truth be told, you just never knew what might happen next. And no matter how long a man worked at the lawdog's trade in the danger-filled, outlaw-riddled Nations, virtually every trip into harm's way offered up at least one event of such peculiar circumstances as to make it remarkable. That surely proved to be the case with Samuel Crazy Snake.

We couldn't have gone more than five miles, a bit north and northwest from the scene of the Dawson gang's brutal murders at the Wilson ranch, when we came upon a sixty-foot-deep, box-shaped depression that appeared to be about a quarter of a mile wide and twice that much long. Picking the killers' trail out of the rough terrain had proven slightly more difficult than we first expected, and slowed our progress more than any of us really liked.

Their track led to a creek off the Washita that cut through the inviting hollow. Lined with cottonwood and oak, the tiny stream dwindled away as it made progress on to the south. Liquid refreshment and abundant vegetation provided innocent traveler and bad man alike with a fine place to shelter from the weather. Every indication was that the murderers had stopped to rest their animals and water up before moving on.

A covered Studebaker Brothers freight wagon sat near the gurgling stream. A rope corral contained six healthy-looking mules. Not more than ten steps in front of the wagon, a white feller had been spread-eagled and staked to the ground.

"Looks like a whiskey deal gone bad to me," Carlton offered. "Probably tried to charge the Dawson bunch more'n they were willing to pay. Then again, they could've simply done him in for the pure meanness of it."

Billy twisted in the saddle and went for his tobacco. "God, I hate these liquor-introducin' bastards. They cause as much trouble as all the killers loose in the Nations."

About then, a tall, lanky Indian dressed in the garb of a Boston banker jumped from the back of the wagon with a rough jug in each hand. Oiled black braids cascaded from under his flat-brimmed felt hat. He held the whiskey containers skyward, whooped and danced his way over to the feller on the ground. There followed some heated, but impossible to understand, yammering directed at the dead captive. Then the dance started up again.

Indian had circled the staked whiskey trader several times when Carlton said, "Think I know the dancer. Bet you whatever we make on this raid, that's a half-breed Comanche feller called Samuel Crazy Snake. He lived in the East with a white family for some years before he came back out this way. He's fairly well known for once-a-year drunken rips and spurts of somewhat peculiar behavior even when sober. Guess he must have had to come quite a distance from his normal stompin' grounds to find a drink. Usually stays to himself over in the Wichita Mountains."

Gently urged Gunpowder down the slope as I said, "Let's mosey in and put a stop to Mr. Snake's ceremonial before he decides to scalp the poor dead slug on the ground."

Carl chuckled. "Oh, I don't think he'd do anything like that, Hayden. Man's pretty well civilized, just drinks too much every once in a while. Of all the Indian drunks I've had to deal with in the past, Crazy Snake's one of the most pleasant. He's about the tamest Comanche you're ever gonna run across. Think he got all his killin' out some years before goin' East."

Samuel Crazy Snake's dust-kicking and foot-stomping continued with a passion. He whooped, hollered, and twirled with such abandon, the approach of three horsed men and two mules completely failed his observation. We'd reined up and spent almost a minute sitting on our animals watching him when he finally noticed our presence, snapped to attention, and looked puzzled. His amazement at our appearance didn't last long, though.

He flashed us a toothy grin, raised both arms, a whiskey jug in each hand, looked to the sky, and said, "Oh Great Father, why do you persecute Crazy Snake so? Now I even fail to spot these clumsy, sneaking white men. Have I fallen so far from your benevolence? What is a poor civilized Indian to do?"

He took a quick hit from one of his jugs, held it out our direction, and said, "You white fellers wanna drink? It ain't very good stuff. Closer to paint thinner than drinkin' liquor. But it'll do the trick in a pinch."

Carlton dismounted. Billy and me followed suit. Crazy Snake didn't wait for us to come to him. He boldly strolled forward and offered the jug again. Carl took it, smelled the contents, and frowned like he'd been slapped in the face with a wet dog. He handed the earthen vessel to Billy, who wet a finger with the liquid inside and tasted it.

"Holy Moses, Snake. Even considering the quality of most of the run-of-the-mill illegal rotgut we get out here, this is some pretty rank stuff. Could well render a man senseless, stupid, and maybe even dead," Billy said, and handed the container back to the swaying Indian.

"Well, it can't make me crazy. I'm already there. Crazy Snake, that's me. A good Comanche man made insane while being raised by white people. I am the unfortunate product of a Methodist education and too much time living in a wooden house, where everything's corners and sharp angles."

I said, "Think I'd dump that stuff. Billy Bird knows bad liquor when he tastes it. Could be nothing more'n wood alcohol. Might kill you deader'n this feller here."

He shook one of the jugs at us. "This stuff can't hurt me. If I drink enough of it, should put me right with the world again. Bet my pony, by the time I get to the bottom of this second one, just might be able to see God." He took another healthy snort. "Hope the ole boy shows up. Been needin' to talk with him face-to-face for a spell now. Some years have passed since our last nose-to-nose dustup. Got a bone or two to pick with the Deity, you know."

I pointed at the poor feller staked out behind him. "Did you kill this man?"

He clumsily twirled around to face the corpse like he'd been hit on one side by something heavy, and swayed like a tree in a stiff wind. "No, sir, I did not. He was extremely dead when I rode up. There was a bunch of horses here before I arrived, though. Look. There's tracks over yonder from six or seven of 'em. Men ridin' in robbed this poor deceased feller blind. These here are the only two undamaged containers I could find. Appears the killers took as they wanted and busted all the rest. Contents leaked all over Hell and gone. Wouldn't let a spark loose around the wagon, if I was you boys."

Billy headed for the wagon while Carl and I examined the corpse. Carl knelt beside the dead man. "Why were you dancin', Snake?" he asked.

"Poor feller went out real bad. All cut open, chopped up, and gutted like that. Bad way to make the trip to the other side. Thought I'd do a short dance for 'im, maybe smooth the path to the other side a little."

"Right nice of you," I said.

He smiled, nipped at the liquor again, and said, "I thought exactly that, my very own self."

"Just out for a drink today, Snake?" Carl asked.

"On my way to visit some folks who live near here, friend Cecil. Accidentally happened upon this poor unfortunate as I passed. Saved me the trouble of looking for him 'cause I was in the market for something to drink."

"Folks you were out to visit wouldn't be named Wilson, would they?" I asked.

A puzzled look flickered across his inebriated, heavily lined face. "How'd you know?"

"Bunch that killed this whiskey runner rubbed out the whole family. We just came from there."

You could hear real distress in the drunken half-breed's voice when he snapped, "Damnation. The Wilsons was mighty fine folk. Nicest people around these parts. Usually visited with them two or three times a year when I came over looking for a snort or two." He shook his head, dropped one jug on the ground, and threw the other against it. "Drinkin's supposed to be fun. Ain't no fun when your friends get rudely murdered."

"No, I suppose not," I offered.

He took his hat off and held it against his chest with both hands. "You boys reckon it'd be agreeable if I tagged along on this raid? Sure would like to see them what done my friends in brought to justice. Certain I could be of some help. Looks to me, from the tracks, you're slightly outnumbered. Another couple of guns can't hurt."

I looked to Carl. He nodded his agreement and said, "He's right, Hayden. Liquor's all gone. He'll sober up soon. Sure won't hurt to have some more firepower. Looks like we'll have our hands full, when we finally catch up with that bunch of killers."

"All right," I said. "You can come along. Stick with Billy. You can help him with the tracking. We sure as hell don't want to lose their trail."

Crazy Snake led a fine-looking pinto pony from behind the wagon. A well-oiled, Yellow Boy saddle gun was nestled in the boot. As he climbed aboard, I noticed a bone-handled Colt beneath his coat that rode high on the waist in a tooled, double-loop,

Mexican holster. It amazed me to admit that as he got mounted, the man appeared to have made a remarkable recovery from the effects of his recent drinking. Then again, like a lot of drunks, he might well have just been highly accomplished at hiding it.

Didn't have time to dig another hole, so we took the dead whiskey runner's grossly mutilated body, loaded it into the wagon, and put the torch to the whole shebang. All that standing liquor exploded in a cyclone of alcohol-fed flame. Burned so hot I could still feel the heat even after we'd moved more than a hundred feet away from the creek. Thick, black smoke billowed into the air, but blew away from us on a favorable breeze.

Carl turned and said, "Hope them boys up ahead don't see that cloud."

Thought about it a bit before I was able to admit to myself he was probably right. Maybe we should have given it some more consideration before setting such a fire. The Dawson gang had already proven themselves to be cold-blooded murderers. Bushwhacking a party of deputy marshals wouldn't concern them in the least.

As Billy and Snake pulled away, I yelled, "Keep a sharp eye out, boys. Don't want any of us to end up like the Wilsons or the whiskey runner."

Knew they would be careful, but a feeling of creeping unease suddenly settled in on me for the first time since we'd left Fort Smith. That kind of gnawing sensation you get when things just aren't quite right, and something on a gut level tells you there's bad times ahead.

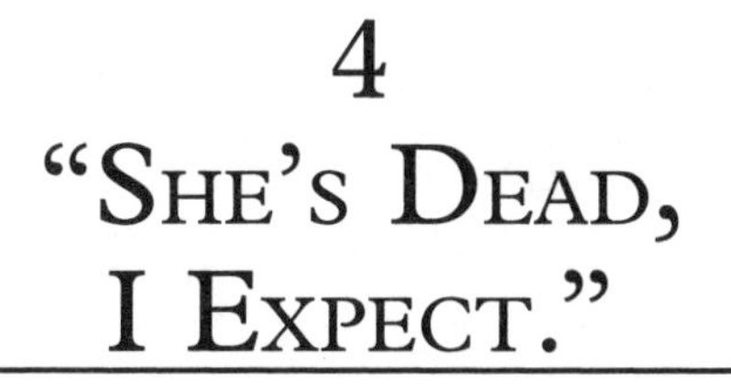

4
"She's Dead, I Expect."

Late the next afternoon, Billy fogged back our direction as fast as his animal could run. Brought the horse to a hopping, clod-slinging stop beside me. He was breathless like he'd been the one doing the running.

"Come quick, Hayden. There's something up ahead you need to see," he said.

Carlton cocked his head like a puzzled puppy. "What? What the hell's got your bob-bin wound up so tight?"

Billy whipped his hat off and wiped his face on the sleeve of his faded bib-front shirt. "Couldn't find no marks on the girl anywhere, but I can't get nothin' out of her neither. Just sits and stares off into nothin'. Damned strange. Gave me the willies just looking at her."

Reached over and took my shaken friend by the arm. "Who? What girl are you rattlin' on about?" I asked.

"Don't know her name. Like I said,

couldn't get her to talk to me. Seems right as rain on the surface, but there's something wrong. Mighty wrong. Got that blank, dazed look you see on people who've had awful stuff happen to them. You need to come quick, Hayden. I left Crazy Snake with her. Maybe you can figure it out."

"Well, lead on. Carlton and I are right behind you, but we can only go as fast as these critters we're leading will allow."

He spun his mount around in a tight circle and kicked away. Handed Carl the line on my mule and said, "No need in both of us tryin' to drag these animals along. Bring 'em up quick as you can. I'll hurry on ahead and see what's got him all humped up and kicking."

"Careful," Carl growled. "Could be some kind of trap, or trick. Just never can be too cautious when you're trailin' the likes of Dawson and Rix."

Followed the swath Billy cut through swaying grass belly high on Gunpowder. Previous trail was easy to retrace as he'd made the back-and-forth trip once already. He managed a quarter-mile lead as we headed over the rolling, almost treeless hills. Three miles or so into the run, a creek slashed across in front of us. Billy disappeared into the canyonlike green cut in the brittle earth's hard-baked skin.

Sparkling clear stream was lined on either side by huge well-watered cottonwoods, blackjack oak, and live oaks. Pulled up beside the largest of the cottonwoods and dismounted near Billy. He stood beside his horse, slapped the reins against his palm, and stared at the base of the tree.

Amidst an enormous pile of brittle, fallen leaves, some as large as dinner plates, the most beautiful Indian girl I'd ever seen sat like a bronze statue. Crazy Snake squatted nearby and shrugged when I walked up, as if to indicate he'd obtained nothing by way of information from her. Billy motioned me forward, but appeared reluctant to approach the girl again himself. As I got closer, her dark-eyed, black-haired beauty became even more compelling.

I knelt right in front of her. Chocolate-colored eyes as big as my thumbnails appeared not to see me. Leaned over as close as I deemed proper. Girl's pupils were drawn up to the size of pinheads. Felt something beside me, and noticed that my companion had reconsidered and now crouched close enough to whisper in my ear.

"Got any ideas, Hayden?"

Picked up a twig and scratched around in

the dirt a bit before saying, "Think maybe she's in shock, Billy. I've seen this kind of hysterical behavior before. Could take some time for her to come out of it."

"Cain't we do nothin'? I mean, ain't there something to remedy the situation?"

"Get a blanket. We'll lay her down, elevate her feet a bit, and keep her warm. Not much else to be done as far as I'm aware. Have to hope maybe she'll come around 'fore morning, and we can find out who she is. Go ahead and set up camp here. We've made pretty good time today. No point pushing it any harder. We'll see what we can do for this unfortunate child."

"Child? Too good-lookin' to be a child, ain't she? How old you think she is?"

Thought I detected some wishful thinking on Billy's part. Typical young-man attitude. "Oh, anywhere from fifteen to twenty. Hard to say, but she couldn't be much older than that. Get me a blanket. Then go help Carl lead the mules in. I'll see to the girl."

He stood, but before taking his leave, bent over and whispered, "She is a beauty, ain't she?"

I stared into the silent girl's exquisitely smooth-skinned, fine-boned, full-lipped face and said, "That she is, Billy. Don't believe I've ever seen another living human being to compare her with."

Me and Snake raked a bunch of the dead leaves into a kind of bed and spread Billy's blanket out over them. Girl made no move to resist as we picked her up and then placed her on the makeshift pallet. Those chocolate eyes closed for the first time as soon as her head touched the blanket. She lapsed into a deep sleep. Didn't move at all before I turned in and headed for a dream-filled night myself.

I awoke to the smell of sizzling bacon, Dutch oven-baked biscuits, and blackstrap molasses. Our recently acquired guest sat on a saddle blanket and wolfed down gobs of food like she'd not eaten in a month.

Carl, Billy, and Snake sipped at their cups and watched the girl from behind the fire circle like a group of curious kids who'd found some kind of exquisite wild animal and weren't quite sure what to do with it.

Poured myself a tin cup of belly wash and squatted with my friends. "Has she said anything?" I asked.

Billy shook his head. Carl said, "Not a word. Grabbed that tin plate out of my hand like she was starved, though. Think if I hadn't let go, she'd of bit my fingers off. I've already refilled it twice. Acts like she ain't had nothin' solid to eat in a month."

Crazy Snake smiled. "Sure as hell got a healthy appetite for such a tiny little thing. Gonna be a big, round woman when she's grown if she keeps eatin' like that. Course I've always liked the fat ones. Takes a woman with meat on her bones to get ole Crazy Snake's attention. One that'll keep him warm on cold nights."

All three of them followed when I strolled over and knelt a comfortable distance away from the girl. She stopped pushing meat and bread into her face and flashed something of a panicked look at us. I waved my friends away, and they quickly scuttled back to the fire.

She went back to eating. "Do you speak English, miss?" I said it low and slow — tried not to introduce any urgency into my question.

She glanced up at me and nodded. Coal-black braids brushed against her chest as her head bobbed up and down. Between biscuit crumbs and half-chewed bacon strips, she mumbled, "Yes. My mother is white. She taught me."

Studied her astonishing face for a bit, and only then detected the presence of some white ancestry. "Where is your mother?"

"She's dead, I expect."

Her response didn't come as much of a

shock. But the possibility of more death ahead still brought a feeling of mild surprise and disgust. "What makes you think that?"

"Bad men came to our house. Killed my father. We heard him yelling outside. Then a storm of gunfire and the yelling stopped. My mother pushed me out the back door and told me to come here and wait."

"How long have you waited?"

The question must have proved something of a puzzle. A thin, long-fingered hand hesitated in midair. A strip of bacon hovered near rose-colored lips, but didn't move for almost five seconds. Finally, she pushed the meat into her mouth and mumbled between chews, "I don't know."

"What is your name?"

Once again, I elicited silence and a blank stare. Near a minute passed before I barely heard her say, as though surprised by the realization, "Moonlight. My name is Moonlight Two Hatchets."

Don't know how in the world Carlton heard what I had trouble making out, but he stood and said, "Are you Jonas Two Hatchets's daughter, miss?"

No surprise in the beautiful Moonlight's voice when she replied, "Yes. I'm Jonas Two Hatchets's daughter."

Over my shoulder, I said, "You know this

child's father, Carl?"

"Sure. Known him for years. Shawnee feller. One of the finest men I've ever met. Thought his place was further north of here a piece. He married a white missionary lady from back East. She was a beauty. Traveled around to all the different civilized tribes preachin' and helpin' folks. Damned fine woman. Now I think on it, this child looks a lot like her mother."

I stood, stared at the numbed girl for another second or so, turned on my heel, and said, "Get loaded up, boys. We need to find this young woman's folks as quick as we can. She says her father is already dead, but maybe the mother is still with us."

Behind me, I heard Moonlight say, "I can't go back there unless my mother comes here to take me."

She seemed determined. But in the end, I forced the issue by making it clear that we couldn't leave her. Hot tears rolled down the girl's cheeks as Billy helped her up behind him. After we'd gone less than a mile, she wrapped her arms around the lanky marshal's narrow waist and appeared to have fallen asleep.

It wasn't all that hard to find Moonlight's home place. Tracks we'd been following, of Dawson and his bunch of killers, along with the smoke and smell of burning flesh, led us right to it. Once we finally had an unobstructed view of the place, I got that creeping sensation, of more blood and death, up and down my sweaty spine. Little doubt existed in my mind that what awaited us in the smoldering ruin, less than a mile away, would evoke more hellish nightmares for years to come.

Noticed, right quick, as how Jonas Two Hatchets had gone a different direction when he built his rustic place. The smoke-shrouded wreck sat on a low hill, and was surrounded by a number of trees that had been set aflame as well. Billy pointed out that the house had once offered a fine view of the surrounding countryside to anyone standing on what was left of a deep front porch.

From a safe distance, Carl stared though his glass and said, "Looks like the kind of home that might belong to a horse trader like Jonas. Newly erected corrals on each side. Pile of scrap rails near the easternmost enclosure. It's empty. Nervous horses in the pen over on the west side. Stacks of new lumber all around. Must have been doing some work on the house. Course, ain't no way to tell exactly what's out back. Stand of oak trees got that part pretty well isolated.

May account for how little Miss Moonlight managed to get away as well."

Billy wiped his brow on the sleeve of his shirt. "Ain't no shot-to-hell bodies a-layin' around in the yard, is they?"

Crazy Snake folded his long glass and said, "Nope. Leastways, I can't see none. Don't mean they ain't around, though. May be hidden, you know. Could be behind the house. Hell, could be anything behind all those piles of lumber and other building materials."

I pulled my .45-70 from its boot and climbed off Gunpowder. Everyone else followed suit. Billy helped the girl down and laid a blanket out for her to sit on. She looked lost, confused, and a bit unnerved. A button-sized tear rolled down her cheek, hesitated as it hung from her jaw, and then dropped to the ground like a lost raindrop.

Billy stared at the girl's damp eyes and said, "You reckon I should stay here with her, Hayden? She ain't in no real good state of mind, from all appearances."

I glanced at Carlton for guidance. He shrugged his approval. "I'd bet Dawson and his bunch are gone by now. Two of us and Snake can take care of whatever we find. Probably a good idea for Billy to stay with the girl, Hayden. Should any stragglers be skulking around, she'll need protection."

So that's the way we played it. Carl, me, and our newly acquired Comanche drifter spread out about ten yards apart and moved slowly through almost waist-high prairie grass. Even though it was the middle of the morning, the wheat-colored stuff was still heavy with dew down close to the ground — soaked our legs and boots.

We came up on the house from the south. Prairie had been cleared away from the building, and we stepped into a well-kept circle at least forty yards from the front entrance. Chills and chicken flesh ran up and down the back of my neck. Overpowering smell from the recent fire gave me a sick feeling in the pit of my stomach.

Bet we hadn't gone five steps when I realized we should have spent a little more time looking the situation over before making a move. 'Bout the time the blasting started, I remember thinking as how we just might have blithely walked into an ambush. Sweet Jesus, that day taught me a hard lesson. Always trust your gut when times are tough. Bastards had laid a brutal trap. First bullet sizzled through the sleeve of my shirt and scorched a path across the hide on my upper arm before I could even react. Next one took my hat off. Way beyond fortunate it wasn't my head.

Then all hell broke loose. Seemed as though Satan himself had personally opened the front gate to the fiery pit and said, "Come on in, boys. I've been a-waiting for you."

5
"Well, Can I Kill Him Later?"

Hot lead bored through the smoke-laden air like angry hornets and fell around us like blistering hailstones. Heard Carlton let out a sickly-sounding grunt as he grabbed at his side and went down on one knee. Dodged from side to side as I ran for the shelter of the ranch's wooden well housing. Dove for safety. Hit the ground hard at the same time Carlton stumbled up and landed beside me.

"You hit?" I yelled over the deafening roar of gunfire.

He held a bloody hand up in my face and yelped, "Son of a bitch knocked a nice-sized chunk out of my side. Had his aim been a little farther over toward my middle, I'd of saddled a cloud and rode off for the Great Beyond."

Grabbed the front of his shirt and rudely jerked him toward me. Snatched the tail out of his pants and eyeballed the wound. He had a nasty-looking black-rimmed hole in the fleshy part of his right side, inch or so above the waist of his pants. Wound oozed dark blood that had already soaked his shirt. Fortunately, in spite of all the liquid he was leaking, the crevice didn't appear to have done any real serious permanent damage.

A wall of heavy-caliber bullets splintered boards, sent dust flying, and made vicious splattering noises on every side of our shelter. Well bucket flew to pieces and landed on top of our heads in a shower of rendered wood and clanging metal bands. Blasting bordered on the thunderous.

"You see what happened to Crazy Snake?" I yelled.

"He headed for the water trough by the corral, over here on the east side. Don't know for sure if he made it, though. Was too busy trying to figure out if I was dead or not. Did you notice anything suspicious, or out of the way, when we were walkin' up, Hayden?"

"Didn't spot a thing out of the ordinary. Sons of bitches were well hidden, I'll give 'em that. I must admit to a creeping sense of impending doom when we stepped out of the tall grass into this open spot, though."

"Same with me. Knew it didn't feel right, but couldn't put my finger to the problem.

Damn, but these ole boys are pepperin' our asses good."

"For all the lead they've thrown, I think you're the only one who got hit. Mighty poor shooting on their part, if you ask me."

Tried to get a peek at who was shelling the hell out of us. Blasting intensified every time I moved and the slightest part of me got exposed. Tiny well house barely offered enough cover to keep us alive. We sat with our backs pressed against it and legs drawn up to our chins.

Tried to pull myself into a tighter knot as I said, "This keeps up they'll chew our protection to shreds — and right soon."

Carl stuffed a bandanna into the cavity in his side, groaned, and said, "Hell, nobody can keep a torrent of lead like this going for very long."

"You get a count on 'em?"

"Sounds like four to me, but could be more — maybe five. Damn, Hayden, this here hole them sneaky jaspers put in me hurts," he said, and groaned again.

Of a sudden, I heard shots coming from behind us and to the west. Carl said, "It's Billy Bird. God help 'em now."

Our friend darted from spot to spot in the tall grass and ripped off shot after shot at our hidden tormentors. Gunfire directed at Carl and me shifted Billy's direction. Gave us a chance to offer up some resistance for the first time. Soon all three of us were pumping lead back at those who'd laid for us in ambush. The tide quickly began to shift our direction as talented marksmen put down a stream of hot return fire.

I noticed that sweet Billy showered a position behind one of the only remaining portions of the burned house that still stood. A heavy, seared, and splintered front entrance door remained erect, held up by what was left of the rendered frame. One of the gunmen, who had taken refuge behind it, switched from side to side, spraying us with well-placed rifle fire. Billy's Schofields couldn't penetrate the thick wood, but my .45-70 could.

When the blasting from our opponents swung Billy's direction, and then began to die down dramatically, I rolled to my side and riddled the thick door with half-a-dozen massive slugs. Heard a screech of agony on the third shot, but added a few more just for good measure. 'Bout then, all the shooting completely stopped, and horses thundered out of the trees behind what was left of the burned-out shell of a house. Billy took out after them on foot, and threw up a running curtain of lead that showered their retreat.

Stood and spotted Crazy Snake, on the ground a bit ahead and to my right, wrestling around on the ground with another man. I yelled, "Don't move, Carl. I'll be back."

Not much strength left in his voice when he whimpered, "Ain't goin' nowheres. Not sure I can even stand."

Darted toward the fight and got there just in time to grab Snake's war-ax-filled hand and stop him from killing his opponent. The man Snake held down was screaming like a gut-shot panther. He could see his own death written in the face of the angry Indian sitting on his chest.

"No," I shouted. "We need to talk to him."

Big half-breed's strength went beyond anything I'd confronted in a spell. Took all I could do to keep him from burying his ax in the terrified man's thick skull. Didn't relax my grip as I pulled him away. Outlaw let out a sigh of relief that sounded like the man's last breath amongst the living.

Both men sucked air like winded racehorses. Crazy Snake shoved the handle of the ax under his pistol belt and said, "Well, can I kill him later? Bastard would've shot me dead if I hadn't grabbed the barrel of his rifle when I did. He was hiding behind this pile of fence rails, Marshal. If he'd managed to kill me, you boys would have found yourselves in a deadly cross fire."

"You fight him the whole time all that blasting was going on?"

"Hell, yes. He's one strong son of a bitch. Went on so long, his friends must have given up on him killing me. They started shooting at both of us like it didn't matter if they rubbed him out too. Wrestled him around on this side to get out from under their guns. Had begun to think he had the best of me. Murderous son of a bitch damn near wore me out. Guess I'm gonna have to stop all my promiscuous drinking. Not good for my endurance."

Wrung-out drygulcher on the ground had fought for his life for so long, he kind of shrank up in exhaustion. Kicked him in the ribs and snapped, "Get up. Not gonna be any sympathy for you here today." He clawed his way to wobbly knees and used the pile of lumber to lever himself to a standing position. I jerked his gun belt off and pitched it to Crazy Snake. Snatched his shirttail out and patted him over for other weapons.

"What's your name, mister?" I asked.

"Watt Sims," he grumbled.

"Ah, you must be the seventh, and unknown, member of this bunch of killers. Where's your pistol, Watt?" I snapped.

"Hell if I know. Big Indian son of a bitch knocked it out of my hand. Fell over yonder by the fence somewheres."

Snake pulled the steel-headed war ax from his belt and shook it in the brigand's face. "Call me a son of a bitch again, you son of a bitch, and I'll split your skull like a ripe melon, whether this high-minded marshal wants me to or not. Then I'll decorate these fence rails with your worthless guts."

Feisty outlaw snorted, "Come over here with that thing again and I'll shove it up your ass sideways. Twist it till you holler."

Crazy Snake's lips peeled back in a snarl. He shoved the ax into his belt again, threw his head back, and before I could stop him, pulled his pistol and shot part of the man's ear off.

Never heard such screaming in my entire life. You'd of thought someone had ripped Sims's entire head loose from his shoulders and set his feet on fire at the same time. He hopped around the stack of fence rails, slinging blood in every direction as he went. Crazy Snake laughed like it was the funniest display he'd ever witnessed. Held his sides and stooped over like he might pass out.

Billy came running from behind the house. "What the hell's going on now?" he yelled.

Snake holstered his pistol. "Oh, nothing. Simply a much-needed lesson for this ambushin' skunk in good manners and how to be properly respectful of his betters."

Ear-shot desperado held a bloody hand over the side of his head and yelped, "Kiss my ass, you red devil."

Billy laughed. "Don't think he learned much from havin' a piece of his ear shot off, Snake."

"Well, I just might have to take off something he values a lot more, next time. What do you say, Billy? Think maybe I should shoot his pecker off?" Half-breed gent flashed a menacing grin, fingered the grip of his pistol, and looked right serious.

Bushwhacker's face screwed up in terror as he grabbed his crotch and turned sideways. "No. Now you marshals cain't let that happen. Ain't right, by God. He's done took a chunk o' my ear. Now he's talkin' 'bout shootin' off somethin' far more important. Just ain't right, by God."

Decided I'd best put a stop to the sport before it got out of hand. "That's enough,

Snake. We're gonna need to talk with this joker later. Billy, you keep an eye on him. Snake, you look to Carl. He's got a hole in his side. I'll check on the one behind the door. Think maybe he's dead."

Billy kicked clods around on the ground. "Well, whatever you do, Hayden, don't let Moonlight get up here and see what's hanging from the trees out back."

Crazy Snake's glance darted to the tall, blackened collection of cottonwoods behind the smoldering wreck of a house. The rise and fall of the property made it impossible for us to see much from where we stood. I could tell from Billy's face and demeanor none of us marshals probably wanted to see what he'd found, either.

As if to himself, Snake said, "Thought I smelled people cookin'."

"Her folks back there?" I asked.

"Both of 'em." Billy pointed toward the center of the stand. "Somebody nailed 'em up to those two biggest trees in the middle. Nasty sight, Hayden. Gotta get 'em down afore she see 'em. They're a bit on the crispy side, as well. Not burnt completely up, but on the way. Maybe we can clean 'em up some, wrap 'em in blankets or somethin' first. No need for the girl to be left with an image of her parents like I just seen."

"No, there's not," I agreed. Waved my rifle at the wounded outlaw and said, "Come with us. Since you probably helped hang these folks up, you can take 'em down."

"I didn't have nothin' to do with that atrocity. Hell, I tried to stop him. Made me sick the first time I seen him go and pull that gruesome trick back down the trail a ways."

"Who? Who're you talking about?" Billy snapped.

"Yeah, Sims. Who're you talking about?" I repeated.

"Nobody. Nobody. Misspoke myself. I wasn't here when those poor people got nailed up and set on fire. Don't know nothin' 'bout it."

So fast I couldn't imagine it happening, Crazy Snake darted to Watt Sims's side, grabbed his hand, laid it on the pile of fence rails, and chopped off two of his fingers. My God, but folks back in Fort Smith must have heard the wailing.

Billy chased Sims around for most of a minute before he was able to slap a piece of rag over the nubs. When he finally got the blood-spurting wounds plugged up, a red-faced Billy Bird turned on Crazy Snake like a tied panther and snapped, "Goddammit, we won't have any more of that kind of brutality. You understand me? Make another move like that and you'll have to deal with me."

Crazy Snake grinned like a fat raccoon that'd just found a big juicy crawdad in a creek. Calm as could be, he said, "Ask him again, Marshal Bird. Ask him who nailed these poor folks to them trees again."

Billy turned on Sims. "Who did it, Watt?"

"Charlie Storms," he yelped. "Crazy son of a bitch done them others, too. Him and Dawson got together and they're a sight to behold. Both of 'em done gone to actin' like they's addled in their thinker boxes." Tears rolled down his cheeks. "Now, they done went and caused me to lose two fingers, and an ear as well."

Snake's grin got larger. "See? All it takes when you want a little information is the speedy application of the appropriate persuasion applied at just the right time."

"Maybe so," I said. "But it ain't our way. Don't do it again. Anything like this happens again, if Billy doesn't get you, I will."

Grin bled away from Snake's curled lips. He snorted in disgust and stomped over to check on Carl. Man mumbled about silly white men the whole time he worked on Cecil's most recently acquired bullet hole.

Billy turned his anger on Sims. "You'd

best not be lyin' to us, you murderin' son of a bitch."

"Ain't lyin'. Swear to Jesus. You know how it is. Two fellers go along doin' this or that. Nothin' real special or bad. One day they hook up, then it's Katie bar the door. That's what I mean about Dawson and Storms. Apart, they're bad enough. Together, those two are a living nightmare. We 'uz all afeared of 'em. 'Fraid they 'uns might kill us if'n we didn't go along for the ride."

Billy stomped away shaking his head and mumbling to himself. He waved a limber hand at Sims dismissively. "That's a total load of manure. Ain't no excuse for this kind of murderous behavior. Fear of the men doin' it's the worst of all justifications."

Sims didn't like it one bit, and I have to admit it was something of a problem with his hand all chopped up the way it was, but I made him pull Jonas Two Hatches and his wife down. We cleaned them poor much-abused folks' bodies up as best we could. Paid special attention to their faces. They didn't look all that bad once Billy got them wrapped in blankets and ready for burial.

Miss Moonlight took it about as well as could be expected. Think the girl had already got herself prepared for the absolute worst possible outcome. Thank God, we'd managed to soften the blow a bit. She wept some, but not as much as I thought she might. Girl kissed her mother's cheek before we put the body in the ground. Child quietly talked to her unhearing father for almost ten minutes before she would let us take him. Sad thing to witness. Had a profound effect on all of us.

Billy requested that I read a passage from Shakespeare to comfort the girl. He suggested a piece from *Julius Caesar* that I'd used many times before. So I read from Act II, Scene ii, "When beggers die, there are no comets seen; the heavens themselves blaze forth the death of princes. Cowards die many times before their deaths; the valiant never taste of death but once. Of all the wonders that I yet have heard, it seems to me most strange that men should fear; seeing that death, a necessary end, will come when it will come." We covered those poor murdered people up and left their daughter to grieve over them in private.

Dead outlaw behind the door turned out to be none other than Harvey Crowder. Moonlight wouldn't allow us to bury him anywhere near her parents. Can't see how anyone would have blamed her for such an attitude. So, we carried ole Harvey's corpse about half a mile away from the ranch.

Scratched a shallow hole in the ground under a big poplar tree and covered him up. No fine words for that bushwhacking swine.

Sims sat near Carlton when the outlaw mumbled, "Better hope his brother Buck don't catch any of you lawdogs out in the open. Buck's damn near as bad as Dawson. Once he finds out y'all done went and kilt his baby brother, ain't no tellin' what he might become." He fingered the bloody bandage on his hand. "Man has an evil temper. I seen him chop a feller's head off with a double-bit ax once. By God, he got my attention. Kept my distance from then on."

Carl said, "Why don't you stop whining. You could have got away from Dawson, and the rest of 'em, anytime you wanted, but didn't. You're just as guilty as the worst of 'em. Judge Parker's gonna hang your sorry self. Best make up your mind to it."

Well, that sobered Sims up considerable. Man didn't have much else to mouth off about. Can't say his surly silence bothered any of us much.

By the next morning, Carl felt a bit better, but needed real medical attention — the kind none of us could provide. We'd done all we knew to do, including upending a bottle of whiskey into the wound and letting it run all the way through him. Billy ground some gunpowder to a fine dust, combined it with some flour, and packed the wound on both sides. Stopped the bleeding, but we were still concerned about possible infection.

My little scratch didn't amount to much, so I told Billy, "We'll hook up some of Two Hatchets's horses to his spring wagon, load Carl inside, and you can take him back to Fort Smith."

"Me? Why me?" Billy grumped.

"Because I'm the only other one who could do it, and I'm not going to Fort Smith," Snake said. "Ain't that right, Marshal Tilden?"

Put my hand on Billy's shoulder. "He's right. Carl needs you to get him back home as quick as you can. It's a big responsibility. He'll be trusting you with his life. I'm gonna keep after the Dawson bunch. Try to kill as many more of them as I can."

"What about the girl?" he asked.

"Take her to Fort Smith with you. She can't stay here, can't go with me, and I have no idea what else we could do with her. She could very well have family around these parts, but right now, I think she'd be better served with some time around more civilized folk."

I've always felt it was the prospect of more time on the trail with Moonlight Two Hatchets that swayed Billy to my way of thinking. Had we not found the beautiful girl on the trail, he would most likely have insisted that Carl make out the best way he could, while we continued the hunt. As it was, Billy set out for Fort Smith less than an hour later with Carl in back of the wagon and the girl seated beside him.

"I'll get 'em to civilization as quick as I can, and ride like hell to catch up with you," he said as I shook his hand.

"Just make sure Carlton gets to a doctor. Drop the girl off with Elizabeth. You'll probably find her at the store. Rest up before you try to make the ride back."

Patted Carl on the shoulder and said, "Take care, old friend. I'll see you in Fort Smith when we've erased as many of these killers as we can from the face of the earth."

He clasped my hand. "Be careful, Hayden. If they'll ambush you once, they'll do it again, or worse." With that, they were gone.

A wounded Watt Sims trailed along behind on foot, his hands tied to the back of the wagon with a twenty-foot length of rope. Man feigned a total lack of understanding as to why we wouldn't let him have a horse.

But since Billy had to make the trip alone, I just didn't trust the outlaw on an animal. Figured he'd try to escape the first chance he got.

As the wagon disappeared, Crazy Snake turned to me and, in a way that gave me the feeling he could read my mind, said, "You don't have any intention of bringing Dawson and Storms back alive, do you, Marshal Tilden?"

"No. I intend to kill all of those left in this bunch as soon as we can catch up with 'em."

He pulled the war ax and ran a calloused thumb along its razor-sharp head. "Ah, now this is beginning to sound more and more like my kind of manhunt."

6
". . . Most Heinous Murders I've Ever Run Across."

Samuel Crazy Snake turned out to be a first-rate tracker and right fine company. He did one hell of a job dogging the Dawson gang's trail north along the banks of the Canadian. The slow-moving river cut through low, rolling, grass-covered hills. Hundreds of tree-lined creeks offered a multitude of steep cuts, sheltered embankments, cliffs, overhangs, heavily wooded ravines, and other such physical features of the landscape as hiding places. The entire area was ideally suited for another surprise attack.

None of the harsh landscape slowed us down too much, at first. We pushed hard for hours. But then, at times, the dense undergrowth slowed us to a walk. As the sun began to set, Snake knelt over the track and said, "We're a lot closer than these fellers expected us to be, Marshal Tilden. They waited around for the remnants of the crew that ambushed us to catch up. The delay has put 'em in something of a bind."

"You reckon they could be hurrying to meet someone else? Maybe pick up a few more guns?"

"Could be, I suppose. No way to tell from the tracks. But I doubt it."

I tried to penetrate the darkening trees, but couldn't. "You reckon they might lay for us again?"

"Maybe, but I don't think so. They're in too big a hurry to get away right now. Doubt they'd stop and ambush us again. No need to worry ourselves about that right now."

"Are they running as hard as it appears to me?"

"No doubt about it, they've put a lot of pressure on their animals ever since escaping from the Two Hatchetses' ranch." He pointed up the steep embankment of a barely trickling stream that ran into the river. "Spurred the poor beasts till they've just about worn them out. Can see where booted men ran alongside the horses up into those trees."

"How much longer before we catch 'em?"

He scratched his chin and stared into the woods. "If our luck holds, and they keep this up, we should be on 'em like ugly on an armadillo by late tomorrow, or early the next day. They're gonna have to stop soon. Animals are about played out for the day and need to be rested. Besides, it's gonna be dark soon. We might as well make camp here. Good water, good shelter, everything a man could ask for."

"Sounds like a fine idea to me. 'Bout wore down to the proverbial nub myself. We can put the boulders under those trees to our backs, picket the horses behind them, and build a fire between us and the water. Should be right comfortable for the night and provide plenty of cover if we need it."

My new traveling partner proved a right fine camp cook, in addition to all his other fine attributes. He combined the best of several different types of cooking — Indian and white. Some of the victuals I couldn't have identified on a bet, but all of them went down easy and settled comfortably on the stomach. Not sure what he did to the coffee, but it was far better than Carlton's ever thought about being.

Once we'd settled in for the night, I managed to gently turn the conversation to an account of his momentous life. He exhibited no reluctance to talk about the events surrounding his past existence, and spoke freely of life occurrences I had only heard about.

He stirred the coals of our fire with a stick and said, "My father was the great Comanche warrior Bloody Wolf. Mother was a captive white woman from East Texas. She was so young when taken, she claimed to have forgotten her name. Only thing she ever told me as a child is that her family lived in Texas, on the Red River near Louisiana. My history is very similar to that of the great Comanche Chief Quanah Parker's. His mother was white as well."

"I must admit to very little knowledge of the Comanche. Came to this job as a recently relocated Kentucky farm boy and have done no study on the matter."

He smiled. Flickering light from the flames danced across his face. "Not unusual, Tilden. Most whites harbor no love for the Comanche. At any rate, I was amongst Quanah's Kwahadies, who came in to Fort Sill with him in June of 1875. I was twenty-two at the time. First twelve years of my life I grew up wild, free, and wonderfully happy. Then, Bloody Wolf got killed in one of the last great Comanche raids made against the whites. Soon as my mother heard the news of Bloody Wolf's death, she grabbed me up and walked all the way to San Augustine, Texas. Next five years were awful."

"Why'd she go to San Augustine?"

"Was where most of her white relatives still resided. Her claims of not remembering any white background proved false. The effort didn't help us much."

"How's that?"

"Took three months afoot to get there from the Nations. Persecution along the way proved very difficult. But once we arrived at her former home, I'm not really sure who treated us the worst, her family, or the other whites who claimed to be *good Christian folk.*"

"In what way?"

"Well, my white grandfather never forgave her for bearing me. According to him, she should have killed herself rather than abide the physical attentions of a *heathen* husband. Only shining light in the whole five years we stayed around that evil old man was the school I attended at the Methodist church. Have to admit there were some right fine people there. Learned everything I could. Soaked up all the white man's knowledge available like a wad of raw cotton."

"You only stayed five years?"

"Yes. My mother died. She called me aside one day and told me she wouldn't be around much longer. Said that once she'd passed, I should pack a bag and go back to the Comanche. Felt I'd be better off with them than the whites. Told me where to look, and who to ask for once I'd found them. Week later, she was gone. Woman just laid down, closed her eyes, and died. Of a broken heart, I think."

"So, you went back to the Comanche?"

"Yes. Walked away from her deathbed and didn't stop walking until I found Quanah and the Kwahadies."

"Have you been happier since leaving the whites?"

"Oh, I suppose. To be truthful, I've never felt altogether comfortable in either camp. And there are others around like me. I've always thought the split we feel in our hearts is what leads half-breeds to often take the wrong trail. Anger, confusion, and drink cause many to go bad simply because they just don't have any idea what else to do."

"If you're at loose ends right now, I can introduce you to Judge Parker. Man of your skills and personal integrity would make a good deputy marshal."

He threw his head back. "Ha, now there's an image for the ages. Sam Crazy Snake a lawman. That, as my white grandfather liked to say, would be a real knee-slapper."

"Might as well be one right now. You're doing the law's work by traveling with me as my posse. When this is over, you'll be owed wages for your services."

What I said must have set him to thinking. For about a minute, the tale of his life ceased. Then he said, "Well, I'd not thought of it exactly like that. Just felt I was helping out a bit. But I suppose you're right."

"Of course I am."

"It pleases me that you have shown such trust in Sam Crazy Snake, Marshal Tilden. Most of Parker's white law-bringers would not have dared trek into the wilds alone with me."

"Oh, I had my reservations, at first. But I want to stop Dawson and Storms before they do too much more damage. After Carlton got hurt, and I lost Billy because of it, you're pretty much a God-sent miracle, as far as I'm concerned."

"Well, you needn't fear anything from most of the peace-loving Indians in the Nations, Tilden. Every one of them knows you're the blood brother of Daniel Old Bear. Should any harm come to Long Gun Tilden, Old Bear's revenge would be swift and bloody."

"Long Gun Tilden? Never heard that one before."

"I knew who you were as soon as I saw that Winchester rifle of yours. Extra-long octagon barrel, flip-up target sights, case-hardened receiver, checkered pistol grip, beautiful weapon. Only one like it I've ever seen or heard of. You, and it, are much feared out here in the Nations, Marshal."

Sound of shod horses coming our direction on the gravel riverbank interrupted our talk. The impossible-to-see threat sent both of us scurrying for safety behind the rocks at our backs. Riders reined up in the fog-laced dark and gloom just outside the light ring of our fire.

"Ah-lo, the camp, me boyos," someone yelled from the shadows. The heavy accent that sounded like a combination of English, Irish, and Texican, plus a thunderous voice, sounded familiar.

"Hello, yourself," I replied.

"Me name's Hamish Armstrong. I be wanderin' if we might share yer fire for the night?"

"Deputy Marshal Hamish Armstrong of Judge Isaac Parker's marshal service?" I called back.

"Aye, 'tis right you are, me bucko. And who might you be, sar?"

"It's Hayden Tilden, Hamish. Come on in."

"Yew wouldn't be about shootin' me now, would you, Tilden?"

"Swear you're safe, Hamish. My partner and I'll hold our fire until I can recognize you."

A massive, mustachioed, bearlike figure that bristled with pistols and knives loomed up on us from the dark and squatted beside our fire. He waved an enormous paw at the pot on the coals. "Would ye be mindin' if I partake of a beaker of your cawfee, Marshal Tilden?"

Crazy Snake pitched him a tin cup. "Help yourself, Marshal Armstrong. Think you'll find it right tasty."

A second man, one I didn't recognize, strolled up to a spot behind Hamish and stopped. Armstrong hooked a thumb over his shoulder. "This hair's me posse man, Pinky Coody."

Coody touched the brim of his peaked cavalry-style hat in greeting as he stepped into the glowing circle of our firelight. Slight of build and clean-shaven, except for an equal number of deadly weapons, he gave the appearance of the exact opposite of his monstrous, hairy companion.

The smaller of our visitors moved to an open spot near the fire, dropped blankets and saddle rolls, and flopped down like a man tired to the bone. Crazy Snake poured a cup of his fine go juice and handed it to our exhausted guest, who sat up, nodded his thanks, and took the brew.

I resumed the comfort of my leafy-soft bedroll. Let both our callers get some of the warm liquid down before saying, "A bit out of your normal range, aren't you, Hamish? Thought you usually spent most of your time up in the Cherokee Nation and over in the Outlet."

"Aye, truly and well spoken, me friend. But we're in parsuit of a heartless killer named Morton Coyle, called Mo by his few disreputable friends. Evil blackguard broke into the home of a Cherokee feller named Thomas Kill Deer. Mardered Kill Deer and then had his way with the mun's wife. Took averythin' he could get his hands on, including the mun's ten-year-old daughter and an extremely valuable blooded harse. We've been on his trail for more'n three weeks now. He linked up with some others a few days back. Evil buggers have been on a killing rip the likes of which I've never witnessed."

Snake said, "They've got a child with them? Now that's a wrinkle I hadn't detected. Be willing to bet you've been coming across burned-out homes and graves."

"Aye. All too horribly true. Number of dead so far is vartually appalling. Pinky's been right careful on the track. Haven't discovered the girl's body along the way. Must assume she's still with him."

The presence of a child in the midst of the insanity we'd seen so far complicated the proceedings and spurred my desire to catch up with Dawson and Storms that much more quickly.

Said, "Well, I think maybe we should join forces, Hamish. Coyle is travelin' with Maynard Dawson, Cotton Rix, Mica Crow Dog, and Buck Crowder. We've been on 'em for some time now. They've left a string of bodies that started with a rancher named Tom Black."

"Heard about that 'un some weeks back now. Mardered the poor man and several members of his unfortunate family, if memory serves."

Armstrong trudged over to his pile of bedding and began arranging it for a night's rest. "Yes," I said, "and a number of others since. You've not heard the worst of it. Somewhere along the way, Dawson and a hard case named Charlie Storms threw in together. According to testimony from a captive, who's now on his way back to Fort Smith, they're committing some of the most heinous murders I've ever run across."

"Jaysus, Mary, and Joseph. What do ye mean by heinous? How might that be?"

"They're crucifying folk, before they set them on fire."

"Crewsifoyin' 'em. Sweet Jaysus. Never heard of such cruelty in all me barn days." He thought that over for a few seconds before adding, "Well, might have to take that 'un back now, yew know. Seen some right awful things while in Her Majesty's service. Especially in the interior of Africa. Yea, it's the God's truth. Some people work real hard at killing their fellow man. Yew're sure about this, Tilden? Ye've seen as much with yer own eyes?"

"I've seen it. So has Snake, Billy, and Carlton."

Pinky Coody spoke for the first time. The man's froglike voice belied his miniature size. "Way I wuz a-readin' the signs, we cain't be very fer behind them fellers. Figured a day or two more to catch 'em."

Hamish threw a few drops of the liquid remaining in his cup on the fire and then pawed around in his bedding. "Well, me boyos, best we settle down for a good night's rest. Long day ahead of us tomorrow, and bad men at the end of it."

Coody and Crazy Snake took turns running the track for the next two days. Hamish and I laid back and tended the pack animals. Trek sped up dramatically when we broke out of the Canadian's tangled bottom thickets just north of Red Rock Canyon. Trail struck out almost true northwest and headed for an area none of us wanted to go.

Our estimates of how fast we could catch up with the murderous bandits proved totally false. Took a spell, but we finally realized our quarry was running at night while we slept. Crazy Snake was the one who finally figured it out. By then, the pack of desperados had put another two whole days between us and them. It was a bitter realization.

We'd all pulled up on one of the low, grass-covered, rolling hills that ran like an endless ocean of seared wheat before us when Hamish said, "Jaysus, Tilden. Would they be goin' to Boilin' Springs, do you think?"

"Sure looks that way. And the way they're running now, I don't think we can catch 'em before they get there."

Coody said, "Boilin' Springs? Is that like them hot springs in Arkansas? Sure would be fine to slip in and take a skin-searin' bath. Got so much dirt on me right now, figure I could raise a right fine crop of snap beans and okra on the back of my nasty neck."

"I'm afraid they aren't like the hot-water springs in Arkansas, Mr. Coody," I said. "Boiling Springs is one of the best sources of naturally fed, fresh springwater for miles around this part of the country. Named the place for the way the surface looks when the water is most active. Water *appears* to be boiling, but it's really only the churning caused by below-surface inflow."

Crazy Snake said, "Streams, ponds, and such from now till we get there are frequently contaminated with gypsum. Men can't drink it. Animals won't go near it. We're gonna have to stop at the first fresh water we can find and fill every canteen and pouch we have. Gonna take plenty of liquid for us and the horses in this heat."

Hamish dipped into a bag of chewing tobacco and stuffed a wad into his mouth. Around the egg-sized gob, he said, "But that ain't the warst of it, Pinky. Bad men from all over the Nations head for Boilin' Springs when they're on the run and intent on seekin' the distant safety of the Outlet. No more lawless spot in the world than the Outlet. When that newspaper bucko wrote as how there's no Gawd west of Fort Smith, he was a-talkin' about the Outlet. Could very well be hawndreds of brigands at the springs when we arrive."

Didn't mean to be heard, but it slipped out anyway. "And every one of them just itchin' to kill any lawman available. You might be right, Hamish. May well develop into an extra-hairy situation, boys. Best get up on our toes right now and stay that way."

"Yew know, Tilden, I've haird some fairly credible tales that Rufus Doome and his insane brother, Jethro, might be prowlin' around these parts. Best be a-prayin' that Dawson and the Doome boys don't manage to throw in together. Such an ugly development could well put us in an absolutely untenable situation."

Hamish Armstrong couldn't have come up with any more potent figures of death and destruction if he'd sat around and thought on the subject for days. The very mention of Rufus and Jethro Doome had the power to send the worst of the worst scurrying into their holes like rats running for the dark when surprised by lamplight. Soon as the names passed his lips, I detected a fleeting look of stunned pain on the face of Pinky Coody.

Crazy Snake pulled an already soaked bandanna from around his sweaty neck and wrung the liquid out before replacing it.

"Well," he said, "sounds as though we've got more'n one yellow jacket nest in the outhouse. Best get primed and ready."

Everyone pulled weapons and checked loads. Hamish, Coody, and I went for our scatterguns. Primed both barrels with buckshot, and rested them across our saddles. No way to know that Death awaited us at Boiling Springs, or that we were headed right into his open, slobbering maw.

7
"Gonna Be Lookin' Up from the Bottom of an Open Grave . . ."

Crazy Snake handed me his long glass. "Wouldn't know any of 'em by sight myself. But I'd bet that's our bunch down there, all right. Only problem is there's at least four more than we've been following. So far, I've counted nine. There could well be more."

Hamish cut loose with a massive wad of reddish-brown tobacco juice spittle that splattered on the hard-baked soil beneath his animal's feet. "Aye. Evil bastards do attract other evil bastards. 'Tis my considered opinion, gleaned from a lifetime of warld travel, they be much like carrion birds — solitary for the most part, they only come together when death and destruction is in the air."

Less than half a mile away, and below us, a stand of seventy-foot-tall cottonwoods teemed with heavily armed men. Located along the banks of one of Boiling Springs's most active small lakes, the Dawson gang lounged in the grass, cooked, smoked, and milled about like a group of church deacons out for an afternoon's fellowship.

I collapsed the telescope and handed it back to Snake.

"Well, what do you think, Marshal Tilden? How do you want to approach this?" he asked. "We know they're bad men. Rank evil to the bone and certain to fight."

Hamish snapped, "If yew're about seekin' council on the subject, Hayden, I'm a-castin' me vote for ridin' down there all guns a-blazin'. Kill as many as we can. Let whatever God those bastards worship sort out them as can save their own worthless hides."

"You sure about that?" I asked.

The giant Englishman grunted and snorted in disgust, "What's to be sure about? We've got 'em by the short and curlies. Stupid bleedin' yahoos have not a clue we're even about. We can ride in and take 'em before they know what hoppened."

Pinky leveled things out a bit when he said, "What about Evelyn Kill Deer? If the child is still alive, and they've got her, she might end up gettin' dead real quick if we ride in there *all guns a-blazin'*, Hamish."

"He's got a point," I said.

"Aye, but it's a chance we're farced to

take, me buckos. We can't be a-sittin' up here in the tall and uncut a-chewin' our ragged fingernails over that poor child's fate. God only knows what harrors those brigands have already put her through."

Crazy Snake pulled his rifle and levered a shell into the chamber. "He's right, Tilden. Quicker we put an end to this, the better for the child, if she's alive, and us."

"Question is, do we try to sneak up and catch them off guard, or mosey up as close as we can, then charge in on them all guns a-blazing?" Once posed, I searched each face for a response to my question.

Pinky answered for all of them. He cocked both barrels on his shotgun and said, "Let's play it exactly the way you said. Mosey up as close as we can. Maybe they'll give in without a fight. Never can tell. If not, we'll charge the camp. Kill as many as we can."

We spread ourselves out so there was at least an eight-to-ten-yard space separating each horse. Brittle, waist-high grass brushed against our animals' bellies as we approached. Nothing seemed amiss, at least not at first.

It was the kind of thing we'd all done before. But for some unknowable reason, about a hundred yards or so from the camp, a sneaking suspicion that something just wasn't up to snuff hit me again. An icy chill ran down my spine accompanied by a river of sweat. And once, when I got a good view into the camp, could swear to Jesus I saw Death, his very own self, grinning and waving for me to come closer.

Couldn't have been fifteen seconds after my creeping premonition of doom that every man in the bandit campsite hopped up with a rifle in his hands and went to blasting. A fiery curtain of hot lead sliced though the prairie grass like a sharpened sickle. Whooping, hollering, and blasting away, like the slobbering inmates from a stone-walled asylum, the Dawson gang laid down an absolutely withering wall of gunfire unlike anything I'd encountered in years.

A blue whistler carved a burning path along the side of my neck at about the same time Crazy Snake's horse squealed and went to ground heavy on my right. I pulled Gunpowder down on his side and got up on my knees to return some of the lead sizzling around us, but the outlaw assault was nothing short of death-dealing. Ammo went through Winchester rifles as fast as they would work the levers. Roar from their direction had all the tempo and speed of a well-cranked Gatling gun.

Off to my left, I heard Hamish yelp at least

twice, but I couldn't see him or Pinky. Killers in the trees kept up their yelling and hollering like they'd just won big bets on a fixed horse race.

Over the din of gunfire, screaming, shouting, kicked-up dust, and the sounds of wounded and dying animals, I heard one of them ambushing snakes call out, "We knew you was a-coming, you badge-carryin' bastards."

Another cut loose with: "We done got you lawdogs this time, didn't we. Made you pay. Made you pay good."

And from another: "Gonna all be lookin' up from the bottom of an open grave in a few minutes, boys."

Bullets hissed through the grass all around me. Don't know how Gunpowder kept from getting hit. I tried to return fire. Set off both barrels of my big Greener. Second time I rose up on my knees, another round peeled the hat off my head and carved a burning crease over my ear, four or five inches long. Nasty wound leaked like someone had hit me with a double-bit ax. Between it and the gash on my neck, my shoulder and right side were saturated with free-flowing blood that caked into an ugly brown mess in a matter of seconds.

The assault finally let up a bit and, in a

minute or so of quiet, I could hear Hamish moaning. 'Bout then Crazy Snake crashed through the grass and fell down beside me.

He popped up on his knees and fired several shots. Got the impression the man was trying to protect me. "You in a bad way, Tilden?" he yelled and fired again.

"Not really."

"Wouldn't know it by looking. My God, man, you've got blood all over you. What about Hamish and Pinky?"

"Not sure about Pinky, but I think Hamish got hit in the first volley. He sure don't sound good."

I turned to speak to Snake directly just as a heavy slug went in one side of his skull and blew a huge chunk of bone, brain matter, and blood out the other side in a rainbow of gore. A puzzled look washed over his face; a faint smile flickered across blood-speckled lips. He went totally limp and rolled over on his side like a sack full of horseshoe nails.

To this very instant, I'm not sure I'd ever been so stunned by a single turn of events. A good man I'd grown to like in a very short time lay dead beside me with most of his brains in a bloody puddle nearby on the ground. Pieces of him were splashed all over me and parts of my horse. So far as I knew,

Hamish and Pinky could have been dead as well — victims of another well-planned and brilliantly executed trap. For the first time in my life, I felt consumed with an overwhelming, uncontrollable rage. Not for certain sure, but think I went to screaming myself.

The shotgun cracked open. Took all my concentration, and most of my reserve strength, to shove two new rounds in and snap it shut. Grabbed Crazy Snake's rifle and stood. Cut loose with both barrels of buckshot as soon as I could see over the grass. Riddled two of the killers less than fifty feet away who'd evidently thought the fighting was over. My unsteady aim proved a little high and both men went down in a spray of bloody mist when the loads caught them full in their faces. Pitched the boomer aside and went to work with the rifle as I advanced on the trees, one stumbling step at a time.

Glimpsed four or five men on horses speed away from the trees in the opposite direction. They left two behind who couldn't get mounted in all the death and confusion. I stopped long enough to take careful aim and dropped one of them just as he got his foot in a stirrup and tried to mount his skittish animal.

Second drygulchin' backshooter surprised me when he pulled a pair of pistols and started my direction, firing as he came. But he was too far away to do himself any good. Let him close the gap by about ten steps, levered a shell into the Winchester, then blasted him out of his boots. Son of a bitch hit the ground like a bag of rocks, snapped back up to a sitting position, and fired several more times. The one I put between his eyes took all the starch out of his arms. Stopped his clock till the Second Coming.

Took two, maybe three, more steps and all the energy drained completely out of my legs. Went down like a felled tree. An oppressive, silent, black hole opened up at my feet and swallowed me like the whale took Jonah.

Not sure how long I was out. Some little while later, opened my eyes and couldn't see anything but white puffy clouds and crystal blue sky. Heard something stir beside me, and turned my head a bit to see Pinky Coody sitting cross-legged beside me. He was covered in streaks of blood, dirt, spent gunpowder, and sweat. A pistol rested loosely in each hand, and he appeared to have been crying.

Surprised him when I moaned and tried to rise up. "Sweet Jesus," he yelped. "Damnation, Marshal, I done went and thought you was for sure dead as well."

Managed to roll onto one elbow. Took a few seconds before my head cleared enough for me to say, "Did they get Hamish, Pinky?"

His chin dropped to his chest. "Guess he was the biggest target them bastards had. Man must have close to a dozen holes in his chest. He was dead afore he hit the ground."

"Crazy Snake went down right in front of me."

"Yeah. I found him, then you. God Almighty, Marshal, you're such a mess and warn't movin' none. I just assumed you was a goner, and that them murderin' skunks had kilt everyone 'cept me." He dragged the sleeve of a ruined shirt across his bloodied brow.

"I think they knew we were comin', Pinky. Laid for us, and nearly killed our whole posse. Can't believe I got suckered a second time. Told myself this would never happen again. Guess the two of us should count ourselves lucky to be alive. What about the horses?"

"Only one that survived was yours. He ain't got a scratch on him, near as I was able to tell. Lot of blood, but I couldn't find no wounds. Guess the blood was yours."

"Or maybe Crazy Snake's. He was right beside Gunpowder when he got hit. Round up all the canteens and get Gunpowder over here. There's a water bottle strapped on his rump. Go up on the ridge and fetch the pack animals down. We always carry a box of medicines, and such, on one of them. Need to get ourselves cleaned up some; then we'll go see how much damage our side managed to inflict."

"Hell, didn't do none I could boast of. Took everything I had at hand just to keep them killers away from me, once my hoss went down. And when the shootin' finally stopped, kept findin' bodies. First Hamish, then Crazy Snake. Thought for certain sure they'd kilt you as well. Jesus, Marshal Tilden, couldn't even begin to figure how I was a-gonna explain this calamity to Judge Parker and the chief marshal back in Fort Smith."

"Don't worry, Pinky. I'll take care of that. Just get the pack animals down here."

He brought me all the canteens he could locate first; then, it took him every bit of half an hour to get back with our pack animals. By then, I'd managed to tidy myself up some. Cleansed my wounds with water and carbolic. Carbolic burned like hellfire and brimstone. Stuff really got my attention when I dabbed some into the nasty gash on my scalp. Pulled a clean shirt out of my saddlebag. Had to throw the blood-soaked one away.

Gore, splattered from head to foot on Pinky, turned out to be from his horse. Poor sad beast got hit in the head and flung the stuff all over him as it went down.

Once we'd got scrubbed up some, I checked on Hamish. Man couldn't have been any deader. Counted eight holes in his chest. Near as I could tell, he never even got off a shot in his own defense. Mighty sad end for a feller who'd traveled the world and fought in countries I'd never heard of before meeting him.

Finally, we eased into the stand of cottonwoods armed to the teeth and ready to kill anything that moved. Of the four men I'd managed to put holes in, all were stone-cold dead, except the yahoo that went down as he tried to get mounted. My staggering aim had been off a mite and I'd caught the poor fool low in the gut. Wadded into a knot over the hole in his belly, he was still alive and suffered mightily because of it.

Knelt beside him and poured some water over his twitching lips till his eyes fluttered open. "Wake up. Ain't gonna let you die yet, you son of a bitch. I want to talk to you some before you shake hands with Satan."

He licked the drops away. "Oh, God," he moaned, "it hurts. Hurts somethin' wicked, mister."

"You should've thought about such a possibility before you started shooting at a deputy U.S. marshal."

"Dawson said you wuz bounty men out to kill all of us. Then when the blastin' started, he and his men went to yellin' 'bout lawdogs, Judge Parker's men, and such. Some of us didn't know you wuz law till then."

"Well, he got part of it right. We would've killed all of you we could. As it worked out, had to settle for just three. Four when you're gone."

He made a weak motion for more water. I let him have one swallow. He smacked his lips and seemed better, but his speech started to hesitate and slur. "Them sorry bastards ran . . . on us. Left . . . us fight their battle. Got me and my . . . pards kilt."

"That they did. Can you tell me your name and the names of your friends?"

Men can last a long time when gut-shot. Almost all I've ever seen died anyway, but, my God, they can cling hard to a fleeting life. Way I had it figured, he was pretty close to shaking hands with Jesus, and identifying the other dead men would help me considerable.

"Name's Elmer . . . Elmer LaGrone. Them three . . . other fellers was Jimmy Martin, Leroy Ply, and Ford Fargo. We weren't . . . bad boys. Just misguided. Led astray by rotten liquor and evil companions. Fell in . . . with the wrong crowd. Ended up getting kilt because . . . of it."

His eyes closed and I punched him on the shoulder. "You know anything about a man named Rufus Doome or his brother Jethro?"

A strange, puzzled look flitted across his twisted face. Could barely hear him when he said, "Heard of 'em. Never met 'em. Don't know 'em."

His eyes closed again and, for a spell, I thought he'd passed on for heavenly judgment and a hell-sent finding of guilt. But he came around again and howled with pain like a kicked dog. After about five minutes of the agonizing racket, Pinky couldn't stand it anymore. He got up and wandered off deeper into the trees. My only remaining partner hadn't been gone more than a minute when I heard a sound from the direction he'd taken that put me in mind of a strangled cat.

Hit my feet running and found him standing over the body of a small girl. "It's the

Kill Deer child," he whimpered. "Sweet Merciful Father, look what them animals went and done to her, Marshal Tilden."

There's no way to adequately describe the horror that poor youngster must have endured — not sure I would, even if I could. Pinky got to heaving and had to stagger from the scene. He made it to a tree, a few feet away, and almost fell down puking. Sight damned near made me sick as well, but I kept the bile down long enough to run back to the pack animals, grab a blanket, and wrap that poor little broken, abused body in it.

Stomped back over to the gut-shot blackguard, grabbed him by the neck, and said, "Who killed the child? You tell me who killed the little girl, and I'll help you on to glory. Clam up on me, you son of a bitch, and I swear to Jesus I'll pile these other bodies all around your sorry ass and ride away. Stinging bugs, maggots, and animals will be on you in a matter of minutes. Wolves will pull you apart limb from limb while you're still alive."

Wild, bloodshot eyes stared into mine. "Coyle . . . and Storms . . . done it," he stuttered. "No one else . . . wanted any part of what they done. It were awful to hear. Feller named Crow Dog even tried . . . to stop 'em. Storms threatened to kill him, too."

He passed out on me again, so I slapped his face till he woke up again. "You're sure about the girl's death? Mo Coyle and Charlie Storms killed her."

"Well, once they'd got done with her, yeah. They're crazy. Craziest living men I done ever seen or heard of. Honest to God, I didn't have nothin' to do with that child's passing." His speech had become slow, halting, and more difficult to understand. Didn't matter, he'd said all he was gonna say.

Pinky Coody's pistol went off less than five feet from my ear. Blast stood me up in surprise like God himself had grabbed my shirtfront and jerked me to my feet. Big .45 slug delivered from an 1875-model Remington ripped though the wretched Elmer LaGrone's worthless noggin and killed him deader than Andy By-God Jackson. Geyser of bright red blood spewed from the hole in his head and sprayed all over the legs of my canvas breeches and boots.

Turned on Coody and started to bless him out good and proper, but noticed a strange, crazed look in the man's eyes. He shoved the pistol back into a crossover holster he wore high on his belly.

"Sorry piece of scum might not have had

a hand in that poor child's unfortunate passing, but he was here and didn't stop it. Makes him just as guilty, as far as I'm concerned. Besides, I'd heard all the whining from the bastard I was willing to listen at."

Couldn't do anything but shake my head. I wanted to tell him he could have at least waited until we'd pumped ole Elmer dry of all the information he was willing to give up. But then I had to admit that I planned to kill the wounded ambusher myself, if he didn't die on his own.

Figured the best way to get Pinky's mind off more murder was to put him to work. Set the example by dragging one of Elmer's dead friends over to his side. Pinky took the hint and, pretty quick, we had all those lifeless brigands lined up side by side.

We dug a hole for Hamish, Crazy Snake, and the little girl under a magnolia tree near the water. Made it deep and covered it with rocks. I was too tired and beat up to read over them.

And when the question of what to do about the others came around, Pinky ended the conversation when he said, "Well, you can bury them it you want, but I ain't gonna help you. Far as I'm concerned the wolves can take care of 'em."

Couldn't blame him much. But I thought it over and came up with a better plan. I pulled some old wanted posters and wrote on the blank side of each, "Ambushing Drygulcher — Killed In The Act." Attached the signs to their vests. Strung all four up from the limbs of two cottonwood trees. I'd done as much before for Comanche Jack Duer and his bunch out on Kingfisher Creek.

Pinky was awestruck. "Now there's a right scary sight. Should be a warnin' to any who'd think about followin' their lead into an outlaw life."

"Well, I hope so. But you just never know. Been my experience, so far, that once a man gets on the owlhoot trail, especially if he descends to rape and murder, ain't nothin' can take him off it but death."

"We a-goin' after them others, Marshal?"

"No, Pinky. Too many of 'em, and I'm whipped. We'll head back to Chickasha. Visit with the sawbones there. Fine feller named Stillwell. Let him check the patchwork we've done on my head. Rest up a few days. Send some telegrams to Fort Smith. Wait and see what works out."

"Sounds good to me. Wasn't lookin' forward to the two of us a-tryin' to bring down the five of Dawson's bunch that's left alive.

Hell, by the time we can catch up with 'em, they could well meet with another crew of knot heads like these we just rubbed out. Nine or ten agin' two ain't exactly my idea of comfortable odds."

Pinky took up a dead man's animal for the one he'd lost — long-legged, bald-faced, blood bay. We struck out for Chickasha soon as we got reloaded and situated. Have to admit, both of us were more than glad to ride away from a bad day at Boiling Springs. I'd seen as many men die at one time before. But the child added an element of horror that didn't want to let go of a seething vengeance growing in my heart. At least we were still alive. More than I could say for those we left behind.

8
"Well, Let's Go Kill the Hell Out of All Them Bad Boys . . ."

Doc Stillwell did a good job of patching us up when we stopped over in Chickasha. He insisted we stay for a spell at his home and recuperate. The robust Mrs. Stillwell, who appeared not to have ever met a biscuit she didn't like, fed us till we almost burst. Hearty lady also made sure we had plenty of water and soap, and even washed all our spare duds. Spent two days loafing around their airy, well-kept home, but by the third morning, I figured it best we be on our way. Pinky agreed.

News of Hamish Armstrong's ambush murder, and the heinous crimes committed by the Dawson gang, traveled ahead of us like waves running in front of a ten-pound stone pitched into a stock pond. By the time we finally got back to Fort Smith, the entire town blazed with righteous indignation over the killings.

Respectable, God-fearing, Christian folk

you'd never have suspected of it sought me out to whisper in my ear about how they hit their knees at night and prayed for the wrath of God to come down on Maynard Dawson and Charlie Storms like a biblical pestilence.

Pinky headed for Jonesborough and the bosom of an anxious family he genuinely missed. He shook my hand before taking his leave. "It was an honor to ride with you, Marshal Tilden. Should you ever need a posse man in the future, feel free to call on me. Be my great privilege to cover your back again, at your earliest convenience."

I stopped over at the courthouse to deliver copies of my handwritten report on both bloody incidents to Mr. Wilton and the U.S. marshal. Marshal was in Washington seeing to the political aspects of a thankless job. Found Judge Parker's chief bailiff in his office.

Wilton's eyes narrowed and he shook his head often while reading my detailed description of the gruesome events prior to, and during, the killings at Boiling Springs. He pitched the papers on his desk and pinched the bridge of his nose in exasperation when finished. Pained expression, of sincere regret, washed over the man's face concerning the whole murderous episode. He appeared especially despondent over

Hamish's death.

Wilton confessed he'd already heard most of what he read in my report. Then, the saddened court officer quietly assured me that he hoped for my quick return to the Nations for some first-class retribution.

"It is never good news to hear that another of our fine, brave men has died in the line of duty. Such information is doubly, perhaps triply, troubling when the man killed is of Hamish Armstrong's caliber. I have, from the first days of Judge Parker's term, always found it extremely difficult to accept such a disturbingly untimely and brutal death."

He stopped, stood, and moved silently to his office window. My secret intermediary with Judge Parker appeared to go into deep thought for almost a minute. He continued to stare out the window, and finally said, as if to himself, "But the Nations is a dangerous place, and being the man who enforces the law of the land, out there, has always been a deadly proposition."

"Hamish was well aware of the hazards he confronted, sir. He exhibited not a single second's hesitation as we charged the Dawson gang. The man just happened to be in the wrong place at the worst possible time."

Wilton pulled the curtain back with his finger. "I have no doubt, Marshal Tilden."

Then, he turned, motioned me to my feet, and escorted me to the door. He shook my hand warmly and said, "Get some rest, Hayden. Take it easy for a spell. Spend some time with your lovely wife. We'll talk about this regrettable mess another day."

Soon as I hit the door, and stepped out of his office, I started putting finishing touches on the plans in my head for how we'd dispatch those killers, when we finally caught up with them again. Ran slap into Billy Bird, as I made my way down the stairs. Memories of Hamish's death, and thoughts on how to deal with the situation, had such a powerful hold on my mind I almost knocked him down.

Man hugged me around the neck like a long-lost brother who'd come back from the dead. Held my elbow and walked me to the door. We stopped in a pool of soul-refreshing sunlight on the courthouse porch that faced the river.

"Good to see you back, Hayden," he said. "Hear tell the Dawson bunch kicked the stuffin's out of you, and them other boys, after me and Carlton had to leave you to your own devices. They even kilt Hamish Armstrong from the sad stories I've heard makin' the rounds."

"You heard right. Hamish died along with

Samuel Crazy Snake. Brigands even murdered that poor Kill Deer youngster — after they'd had their way with her."

"I'll just be jiggered. Hadn't heard about Snake. Kilt him, too, huh? And the little girl as well. Jesus H. Christ, what are some men in this world coming to?"

I pulled him to a more private spot behind one of the porch pillars. "Those cave-dwellin' rats shot Carlton, killed Hamish, Crazy Snake, and the little girl, and left bodies nailed to trees all along their bloody trail."

"True. All too true, Hayden. They done some of the worst murders I've seen since coming to this work. Would imagine you have plans in mind for 'em by now. Leastways, I sure hope you do."

"I've had plenty of time to think on the subject, Billy. Soon as Carl's up to it, the Brotherhood of Blood is going back out into the Nations after those bastards."

"Sounds good to me."

"Be aware that I don't care where we have to go, or how long it takes. I intend on bringing down the wrath of God on the heads of Dawson, Storms, Rix, Crow Dog, Coyle, Crowder, and the Doome boys, if they prove a part of this."

"Even if we have to go to Texas, New

Mexico, or other such places?"

"Even if we have to go to the front step of a smoldering hell. Those killers are gonna pay with their sorry lives for what they've done, if I have to ride into fiery Perdition myself and shoot the horns off a scarlet Satan. Tell you the truth, my friend, I've killed my share of men over the years, but this is the first time, since I watched Saginaw Bob swing from Maledon's gallows and mess his pants in front of a thousand people, that I'm gonna take considerable pleasure in other men's departures from this life."

Billy fingered the walnut butts of his Schofield pistols and smiled. "Love it when you talk that way about rubbin' out human scum, Hayden."

Of a sudden, the face of Moonlight Two Hatchets popped into my mind. "How's the Two Hatchets girl doing?"

"Can't say. She wouldn't come to Fort Smith with me. Made me stop over in Minco Springs and drop her with some relatives. Has an uncle livin' there." He looked some distressed, for a second or so. "I know you told me to bring her to Elizabeth, Hayden. But she just wouldn't come. And you know how it is with me and beautiful women. They get to cryin' and I cain't refuse 'em anything."

"You sure she's safe?"

"Oh, yeah. Her uncle was a stand-up feller name of John Little Wolf. Me and Carlton stayed over at his place for three days. Little Wolf helped Carlton out a bunch. Not sure he'd of made the whole trip without us stoppin' along the way somewheres."

"How's Cecil doin' these days, Billy?"

"Feelin' right sparky. Hole in his side wasn't nearly as bad as it looked. He's done went and got plenty of rest lately. Think maybe his wife loved him up pretty good, too. Another week, or so, and I figure he'll be sloshin' over with piss and vinegar — hotter'n a two-dollar pistol in a Fort Worth whorehouse and ready to ride again. And you know how he is when he gets that way. It'll be Katie bar the door when we catch any of the devils that kilt Hamish."

Guess the relief must have showed on my face. "That's great news, Billy. Good to hear he's doin' so well and that Moonlight Two Hatchets got back to her family. Must admit, I have been some concerned about Carl."

Billy grinned and patted me on the arm like he was my mother. "Ole Carlton's been stewin' over who put that hole in his hide ever since we got back. Told me he'll kill the son of a bitch, soon as he finds out who done it. Knowin' Carl, he just might even rub out a dozen more who didn't have anything to do with the shootin', just for the pure-dee ole Carlton-J.-Cecil-mean-assedness of it."

"I'm heading over to the store to visit with my wife for a bit. Then, I'm gonna take her home and den up for two, or three, days. So don't come looking for me until Friday or Saturday."

As I stepped into the stirrup and hoisted myself up on Gunpowder's back, Billy puffed a hand-rolled to life, and flicked the match away. "I'll send some telegrams to all the Light Horse, sheriffs, and Indian police in the Nations, Hayden. We should be able to scare up some kind of information on the Dawson bunch between now and then. I'll bring Carl with me when I come out."

"Good. If you run across Carl before you boys make it out my way, tell him it had been my intention to come by to check on him to make sure he was all right. But, since you assured me as how he was alive, kicking, as bold as a six-time bigamist livin' in the same house with three of 'em, and ready for a fight, I decided to wait."

As I kicked away, Billy waved and yelled, "I'll tell him."

Made my way through all the hustle and bustle along Fort Smith's Towson Avenue. Had to carve a path through a heavy cloud of drifting dust that hung in the air till I got to the store. It appeared as though Elizabeth's permanently employed painter had taken a healthy swipe at the Colonial-style pillars out front. My God, but my wife kept that poor man running, what with all her different businesses.

Elizabeth had this thing about "shabbiness." Always said there was just nothing like "shabbiness" to turn off the female shopper. Master painter Jimmy Osborn spent virtually every waking moment of his life slapping a new skin on something my wife owned.

That hard-working gal of mine claimed that lack of a "prestigious" appearance had the exact same effect on those who frequented the bank her father left us when he passed. As a consequence, Fort Smith's Elk Horn First National presented the outward show, and the inward reality, of being one of the most celebrated financial institutions to be found anywhere in the entire nation. Sign over the president's desk read, SAFEST BANK WEST OF THE MISSISSIPPI. And I suppose it was. Elizabeth Tilden's financial establishment had never been robbed, and no customer had ever lost a single cent in deposits. Mighty fine record, if you ask me.

Cute little flirt of a clerk at the store batted big blue eyes at me and cooed, "Oh, Mrs. Tilden went home for the day, Marshal. Said she felt like taking the afternoon off." Girl ran her finger around on the counter and acted coy. "Can't say as I blame her much. I'd take the afternoon off myself, if I could."

"Well, Millie, if it was up to me, I'd let you have the rest of the day to do a picnic out on the bluff with your favorite feller. But, as you are probably well aware, my say around Miz Tilden's businesses is about as worthless as trying to speak Chinese to a box full of rabbits." She went into a giggling fit as I tipped my hat and headed for the door.

Elizabeth must have spotted me coming up the hill, a quarter of a mile from our house. She burst from the front door, sprinted across the deep, covered veranda, and ran down to meet me. Beautiful girl threw herself against me with such abandon, when I stepped off Gunpowder, she almost knocked me down. Then, she slapped a big wet kiss on my mouth that near turned me inside out. Rowels on my spurs went to spinning by themselves and, for a second, I would've sworn steam rose from the collar of my shirt.

She broke the kiss, snatched my hat off, and said, "Oh, my God, Hayden. Your telegram said you'd been injured, but darlin', that is one nasty-looking crease in your scalp." She pushed my head around with her finger and gently traced the black-scabbed wound on my neck. "Sweet Merciful Father. This one is almost as bad. Does it hurt?"

Hugged her close and said, "A little. But you needn't worry, darlin'. Doc Stillwater, over in Chickasha, sewed me up just fine. He seemed pretty sure I'll heal up so fast you won't even remember these little dents in two or three weeks. I should be able to cut the stitches out in a few days."

Her head fell on my chest and she sobbed. Knew I'd probably hear the "We're the wealthiest family in Fort Smith; you don't have to put your life in jeopardy if you don't want to" speech before everything calmed down some. But she didn't say anything. Just let out a pair of muffled sobs, and then perked right back up and went to smiling again.

She shoved her hips forward and rubbed against me in the most provocative manner. Sultry as a summer night in New Orleans, she said, "Guess I should thank God those bad boys weren't shooting low." Then she bit me on the ear and whispered, "I'll race you to the bedroom, handsome."

That afternoon, and all that night, Elizabeth made love to me with an abandon that almost caused the wax to pop out of my ears. We'd been trying for over a year to have another baby. I truly thought that after our son, Tommy, passed, Elizabeth might not want another child for sometime to come. But she put that silly notion to rest in pretty short order. Most beautiful woman I knew informed me in smoky-eyed, passionate word, and deed, that most of my free time away from the Nations would likely be spent in blazingly carnal efforts designed specifically to produce another chubby-pink Tilden, as quickly as possible. Truth be told, it got to a point where it was impossible to keep clean sheets on our bed, anytime I managed to spend a few days at home. God Almighty, sometimes that beautiful gal's unbridled passion seemed to have no limits.

But the next day, she tore herself out of our bed and went back to her businesses. Such behavior was typical of the girl. As she always said, "Love is love, and sex is sex, but business is business."

Third day after I got back, Carlton and Billy moseyed up a few minutes before noon. I was really pleased to see Carl. Hugged him like family and looked him over real good to make sure he wasn't just putting on a show of feeling better. We sat on the veranda, drank big glasses of lemonade in the shade, and feasted on the beef, onion, and tomato sandwiches Elizabeth made before she headed for town that morning.

Carlton provided the cigars, and I cooked some coffee after we ate. We were sprawled in our chairs and blowing smoke rings when I said, "You're looking fine as dollar cotton, Carl. Guess that hole the Dawson bunch put in you didn't do as much damage as we first thought."

"Big chunk of burnin' lead went all the way through me." He lifted his bib-front shirt and pointed at the red weal a few inches above a pistol belt that was decorated with solid silver Mexican conchos. "Poor-shooting son of a bitch only managed to get this fleshy part of my side, thank God. Little more towards my middle and whoever got lucky enough to hit me would probably have kilt me deader'n a fifty-year-old petrified hoe handle."

Billy chuckled and snorted, "Hell, Carl,

thin-as-a-rake feller like you has gotta consider hisself mighty lucky. No more fat than there is on that stringy behind of yours, it's a wonder that bullet didn't blow you in half."

Carlton feigned indignant offense. "By Godfrey, I do consider myself lucky, Mr. Billy By-God Bird — real lucky, as a matter of plain fact. All I want now is the chance to even up the score a mite. Maybe put a mark or two on whoever done this to me."

I offered up a smoke ring the size of a number-ten washtub that floated Carl's direction. Thumped a pile of fine-smelling gray ash on the ground and said, "Well, you're about to get a chance to do exactly that, if you're as game as you make out, Carl. Billy and I've agreed that we're gonna go after them boys again. I intend to rid the world of Dawson and his bunch once and for all — no matter what, or how long, the bloody chore takes. Spent most of my time thinking about those murdering polecats all the way back from Boiling Springs."

Billy puffed at his smoke and spit out a sprig of tobacco. "You and your posse had a bad day at Boiling Springs for damned sure, Hayden."

"Yep, real bad, Billy. Bad as it gets. Maybe if you boys had been with me, the whole deal would've worked out a bunch different. But you just can't ever tell. I've been thinking that this is still a job for the Brotherhood of Blood."

Carl took a long drag on his stogie, then held it up as though examining the burn to make sure it was even. "Ain't gonna try to bring any of 'em back this time, either, I take it."

"You take it exactly right, my friend," I said. "As both of you are already aware, I never intended to bring any of them back alive to begin with. Judge Parker sent me out to kill 'em the first time around. Our plans just didn't work out the way I intended, or expected."

Billy pulled one of his Schofield pistols, broke it open, and examined the loads. "Well, I can tell you for sure, there ain't gonna be no third time with any of this bunch. I got word yesterday, from an old amigo of mine over near McAlester, that he'd spotted Mo Coyle and Buck Crowder. We get to humpin' it right quick, should be able to catch them bad boys unawares before they can get away again. According to my friend, they're pretty heavy into their liquor these days. Given the crimes they took part in, such behavior could well be an effort to drown a right bothersome conscience."

"You hit that 'un on the head. Bet God's a-troublin' them considerable over all the terrible things they went and done, or was party to, while ridin' with Dawson and that lunatic Charlie Storms," Carl said.

Had to shake my head when I recalled the death and destruction we'd found in those outlaws' wake. "Don't get much worse than nailin' people to trees, settin' dead bodies on fire, or child rape and murder," I mumbled.

Billy scratched his chin and looked lost in thought. "Just how far are you willing to go to get this bunch, Hayden?"

"We'll do whatever's necessary. And I do mean every word of what I just said. There won't be any soft glove for those who might have information, either. You understand?"

Billy nodded. Carl grinned like a fox loosed in a henhouse. For about ten seconds, no one spoke. Then Carl said, "Well, let's go kill the hell out of all them bad boys we can find, fellers. That way they won't never do nothin' like we seen again."

9
". . . Cut Ole Selby's Head Off and Stuck It on a Pole . . ."

Just to prove that nothing ever comes as easy as you hope, it took us a goodly amount of investigatory, lawdog-type snooping, in some of the rougher parts around McAlester, before we ran Mo Coyle and Buck Crowder to ground.

Prez Tate, a good friend and former drinking buddy of Coyle's, finally turned loose of the fact that they'd put up in a shotgun cabin beside Wild Cat Creek, up on Pine Mountain. I say finally, because it took more than the usual amount of persuasion to convince the liquor-saturated slab of sorry bar-squeezin's just how serious we were.

We caught Prez outside an illegal whiskey peddler's place south of town, just before dark, about a week after we left Fort Smith. The drunken lout was a former buffalo hunter and, at one time, could have easily boasted of being tougher than a Comanche quirt made out of chewed rawhide. But time, risky behavior, and a raging river of highly questionable, bonded-in-the-barn jig juice had turned the man into an unshaven, stinking heap of quivering, fringe-covered filth unfit for most human companionship. Not sure he had a living friend within a thousand miles of the Nations.

Drunken scum yelped like a stomped cat when Carlton gave up on all the worthless talk and said, "This is just to let you know that we're as serious as malaria about wantin' to know the whereabouts of Coyle and Crowder, Prez." Then, he grabbed the foul-smelling mound of human waste by the ear and lopped a little bitty chunk of the lobe off. Really wasn't much more than a nick. But you'd of thought Carlton cut the stinking bastard's entire head off.

God Almighty, the sorry besotted skunk couldn't talk fast enough after that. Even drew us a map on the back of a John Doe warrant of how to find Wild Cat Creek and the cabin where he claimed Coyle and Crowder were holed up.

He handed the paper to Carl with a quaking hand and sniffed, "Sweet Merciful Father and heavenly choirs of angels, ye didn't have to cut me ear off, ye badge-totin' son of a bitch."

"Didn't. Only took a piece of that unimportant dangly part," Carl said. "Now, if you'd like, I could whack off a smidgenly portion of the other'n, so's they'd match up."

Tate covered his good ear and yelped, "No, damn ye! Ain't no need. Hell, ye didn't have to do the first'n. I'd of tole ye what ye wanted to kin eventually."

Billy pushed the butts of his Schofields forward, dropped his chin on his chest, and looked doubtful. "Well, now is that a fact? You would have talked right up for the price of a jug of giggle juice?"

Tate looked hurt, like it pained him immensely that Billy didn't believe him. "Hell, yes. If'n ye'd of just bought me a nice jug of whusky, I'd of spake up right off. No need fer bloodshed — 'specially mine. I can be right cooperative with you law-bringin' fellers, if'n the proper enticement is to my likin'."

Billy threw the rancid pile of human debris a bandanna for his leaking ear. "We don't have time for deal-makin' with the likes of you, Tate. Coyle and Crowder are sought for the worst kinds of wicked murder. This ain't like horse stealin', petty thievery, or introducin'. We want these two low-life sons of bitches — real bad."

Carl wiped the blade of his razor-sharp

bowie on the leg of his breeches. "And we aim to get 'em, no matter what that involves. Come down to it, I'd of relieved you of everything stickin' out where I could lop it off, for the right information."

"Yeah, well, that shouldn't include whackin' off a law-abidin' citizen's hearin' equipment. Just might have to take you fellers to court for damages," the smelly ruffian whimpered.

Carlton leaned down into the inebriated yahoo's face, thumped him good and hard on his damaged ear, and said, "If you show your ugly mug in Fort Smith all bathed, cleaned up, smellin' of lilac bathwaters, sportin' a new suit, and in the company of some slick-talkin' lawyer, someone's gonna find your much-abused body out by the town dump the next day. I can personally promise it'll be missing some extremely vital pieces you're not gonna like partin' with." He whipped the bowie around and flicked the tip against the crotch of the whimpering sot's pants.

Tate looked stricken. "Sweet weepin' Jesus, calm yerself, Marshal. Ye don't have to get so all-fired excited. I wuz jest rattlin' off at the mouth, as it were. Didn't mean narry a thing by my jawin'. Ye don't be havin' to worry none 'bout ole Prez Tate a-showin' up with no slick-tongued lawyer. Swear to Jesus. Never happen. Not in this life, I gar-n-tee."

I held out a spanking-new ten-dollar gold piece so he could see it. "Are you sure Coyle and Crowder are where you said they are, Prez?"

He eyeballed the coin and went to drooling like a man about to be made wealthy beyond his wildest dreams. "Yessir. Absa-damn-lutely. They be on Pine Mountain exactly as that 'ere map I done drawed fer ye indicates." He held up his right hand like a witness in Judge Parker's court. "God be my guide. Ain't tole you boys nothin' but the hull truth, and nothin' but."

"Are they alone?" I rolled the coin over my fingers, so the dying sunlight made it sparkle and shine.

He looked confused, scratched a scraggly chin, and cocked his head to one side like a dog listening to its master read instructions from a book on the intricacies of algebra. "Well, now, that 'ere particular piece of information might be worth more'n ten dollars, Marshal."

Carl whipped out his razor-sharp blade again. "Is it worth more'n a big chunk of your other ear, or maybe your nose, Prez?"

Tate slapped his hands over both sides of

his head, turned away, and whined, "Wait, wait, now. No need to go and get all hot and bothered again. They might be one other feller with 'em. Could well be as how they done picked up a compadre, as it were."

Billy peeled some of Tate's fingers off an ear, leaned close, and said, "And who would that other feller be, Prez?"

"Well, I ain't sayin' for certain sure, Marshals. But it may possibly be" — he drew it out for several seconds before finally saying — "Selby Hillhouse." He took a sneaky glance at each of our faces. Always felt the man wanted to make sure his stunning announcement had the proper impact. It did.

Carlton shot a glance at me. "Did you hear that, Hayden? Selby Hillhouse himself, no less."

Billy shook his head and slapped a quirt against the leg of his chaps. "Sweet Merciful Father. I ain't heard that name in at least three, or four, years. Thought somebody killed his sorry, murderin', thievin' self down in Texas. Heard them Texas boys cut ole Selby's head clean off and stuck it on a pole outside San Angelo after he went and rudely murdered one of the town's leading citizens."

Prez smiled like a snake in a henhouse full of newly laid eggs. "Well," he said, "guess ye'd be wrong 'bout that 'un, Marshal Bird. Done seen him with my own eyes. He's very much alive, and he's twice as mean and ugly as ever. Gonna take all three of you boys to throw a loop on a killer like Hillhouse. Coyle and Crowder, now they's bad enough. But Hillhouse? Just thinkin' on the man is enough to make my blood run colder than clear mountain streams in the Rockies after the thaw."

Pitched Tate the coin and left the poor wretch chuckling away at the information bolt from the blue he'd dropped on us. Headed for Pine Mountain as fast as good horses could run. Got to give credit where credit's due. Every cell of Ole Prez's sorry body might have been saturated with cheap, brain-burning panther sweat, but he could still draw a mighty fine map. 'Bout noon the next day, we found Wild Cat Creek and the coarse cabin exactly as he'd marked it down.

Board-and-batten building was constructed of weathered, rough-cut pine planks and sat on a small rise forty or fifty feet from the freely running stream. Backside of the shack appeared to have been part of an original dugout shelter carved into a rock-covered mound. Lean-to shed, on the end away from the water, provided refuge for three horses held in a rope corral. Massive cottonwood stood between the front corner of the building and the creek. Covered belt-buckle deep in big bluestem grass, and treeless, the sloping area between us and the cabin offered little by way of discernible cover from any gunfire directed from inside the rickety structure.

We reined up behind a knobby hill, about a quarter of a mile away from our objective. Tied the animals below and crawled to the top. Laid on our stomachs and passed Billy's long glass back and forth as we studied how to go about smoking the murdering scum out of their hidey-hole.

Carl said, "Ain't gonna be easy, Hayden. Not much of anything to take cover behind, between here and there. Course they'll have a tough time spottin' any of us in grass this deep — as long as we don't move around much."

"Might have to burn 'em out, boys," Billy offered. "One of us could sneak around to the backside. Gather up some grass and twigs along the way. A feller can almost walk right out onto the roof from the rocks behind the place. Get a good spark goin', and I'd be willing to bet those dried-out pine wall planks will go up like sun-bleached tinder and firecrackers."

About then, the cabin's leather-hinged door popped open. Someone staggered backward onto the rickety porch. The obviously drunk bandit carried a jug under one arm and pointed into the darkness of the gaping entryway. He yelled like a man in violent conflict with a person, or persons, unseen, but we were too far away to make out exactly what he said.

Billy slapped the collapsible scope up to his eye and stretched it out to its optimum length. "That's Mo Coyle," he said. "Looks to me like he's gettin' disputatious with someone inside. Goin' at it pretty hot, too. Man's mighty upset about something. Whoa, momma. Clumsy jackass just stumbled backward down the steps. Aw, now that's too bad."

"What's too bad?" Carl pawed at the telescope, and finally pulled it out of Billy's hands. He squinted through the eyepiece and said, "Ha. He fell on his jug and broke it. God Almighty, he's madder'n a nest of stirred-up hornets now. Really givin' someone inside a serious cussin'. Uh-oh. Look in the doorway, boys. That's none other than Selby Hillhouse, his very own self, standin' there. He don't look none too happy, neither."

I said, "I've never seen the man before, Carl. Come on, now. Gimme a little look-see."

Cecil reluctantly gave up the long glass. "Big ole boy, ain't he. Must be every bit of six-and-a-half-feet tall. Has the kind of face that makes you think he could probably bite the head off a hammer and spit out a pound of tacks."

I watched as Coyle continued to shake his finger and yammer at the huge man who loomed above him on the porch. Hillhouse didn't say much in return. As nearly as I could tell, he appeared nigh on bored to death with the mouthy ruckus. Coyle got madder and louder, the longer he ranted. Grabbed up chunks of his earthen jug and shook it at his seeming tormentor.

Guess Hillhouse finally got all the angry, curse-laden lip he wanted to hear. Long-barreled cavalry-model Colt flashed out of a cross-draw holster and delivered a booming chunk of hot lead that, on first impression, appeared as though it hit Coyle in his right leg. Coyle hollered so loud, it sounded almost like he was standing right beside me.

Billy snickered and rolled onto his back. "You know, it could well be, if we wait long enough, these idiots will kill each other off. We won't even have to expose ourselves to the trials and tribulations of gettin' them fellers to give it up. Just lay up here, take a nap, while they murder one another."

"Sounds good, Billy. And the God's truth is there's just nothing I'd rather witness. Always better not to confront killers and gunhands like these if we can pull it off. But I think you're forgetting something real important," I said.

"What?"

"We need to talk with either Coyle or Crowder. Really doesn't matter which one, but we don't want both of 'em dead until after a little heart-to-heart chat."

"Why?"

"Quickest way we're gonna find their running buddies, Maynard Dawson and Charlie Storms, is to get it out of the poor idiot rolling around in the dirt, or his friend. Now, Hillhouse is another story. Maybe we should all hit our knees, offer up some serious prayers that he ends up dead before we have to go down there. 'Cause if the stories I've heard are even close to being true, I'd rather not get into a toe-to-toe gunfight with the man if it can be avoided."

We continued to watch the show, as Coyle flopped all over the dusty ground and screeched like a turpentined cat. Hillhouse waved his pistol, and said something right pointed to the wounded gunman. After a bit, the infamous shooter of men holstered his weapon and disappeared back inside the shack. Second or so later, Buck Crowder came slinking out the door and hustled down the steps to help his wounded compadre.

Carlton said, "Ain't no two ways about it, we're lookin' at one lucky man."

"How's that?" I asked.

"Well, from all the tales I've heard, if Selby Hillhouse pulls a pistol, he usually leaves a seriously dead, leakin' body behind. Guess maybe he must like ole Mo some. Otherwise, he'd of killed the poor leg-shot chucklehead deader'n a rotten stump."

Billy snickered. "Even so, there is a good side to what just happened, Carl. They sure don't seem to have their minds on the possibility that the law is creepin' up on 'em. Such ignorance should work to our advantage."

Crowder eventually got Coyle up on wobbly legs. The wounded man leaned on his friend and hobbled back into the cabin holding the spot where he'd been shot. Carlton observed that Coyle didn't appear to be bleeding very much, which, in his opinion, simply confirmed his theory that Hillhouse hadn't really intended to hurt the loudmouthed drunk very badly to begin with.

Carlton struck a thoughtful pose and said, "Selby Hillhouse ain't no slouch with a pistol. If'n he wanted Mo Coyle dead, you can bet next month's pay Coyle'd be shakin' hands with the devil and makin' arrangements for a room in a flaming perdition right this minute."

Billy slapped him on the back. "Well, that's good to know, Carl." Then he pulled a pistol, checked his loads, and said, "But, fellers, ain't nothin' we're doin' right now that's gonna bring this dance to a close. So, I reckon as how we'd best stroll on down there, let 'em know we're here, and that their days amongst free men are over and done."

Took us a few more minutes to pull a shotgun and rifle apiece, make sure we had plenty of shells, and decide who would circle around to the backside of the shack and set the place on fire if necessary. Carlton got the short straw on that one, too. He flicked it away and looked disgusted.

"Damnation," he grumped. "If it weren't for the fact that you're the feller who always holds the straws, Hayden, I'd swear this deal was fixed. Think this is the fifth, maybe sixth, time I've done went and drawed the short one."

Billy clapped him on the back again and said, "Don't forget the grass and twigs, short-straw man. You'll wanna get their attention with that fire as quick as you can, oh, great and sneaky one."

Pulled both of them close. "Be careful, boys," I said. "Don't want anything to happen that might get one or more of us killed today. There's at least three desperate men down there just waiting for the law to come along and gather them up. Kill 'em if you have to, but remember, we need Coyle, or Crowder, alive, if possible."

10
"You Didn't Have to Set Me on Fire . . ."

Carlton nodded and stumbled away from my spur-of-the-moment meeting, mumbling something about, "Just ain't natural, that's all. Cain't get the short straw every damned time. Hell, it just don't make any sense. Law of averages says I've gotta get a long one sometime or t'other."

Me and Billy set to crawling our way through the windblown grass. Had a stroke of good fortune once we got to the edge of the heavy growth of big bluestem. Nice-sized horse trough and water pump we couldn't see from the hill gave us a little something to hide behind, thank God. Wooden tank appeared to be new and constructed out of heavy two-by-twelve boards.

Got set up. Kept as quiet as we could while we waited for Carlton to get ready. Once he waved from the rocks behind the shack, the whole square dance, doo-dah show, and perambulating parade got to moving pretty fast.

Billy ripped the rag off the bush a bit quicker than I really wanted when he yelled, "Mo Coyle, Buck Crowder, and Selby Hill-house, this is Marshal William Tecumseh Bird speakin'. You belly-slinkin' bastards are surrounded by a heavily armed company of deputy U.S. marshals from Judge Isaac Parker's court in Fort Smith." Then he turned to me. "You yell out now, Hayden. They'll know there's more'n one of us."

So, I hollered, "We have official court warrants for the arrest of everyone of you. Come on out with your hands raised, palms up, holsters empty."

For about ten seconds, nothing happened. Got quieter than a deaf mute's shadow. Thought I could hear my hair growing. Grass waved behind us and sounded like a pretty girl's petticoats swishing down the boardwalk in Fort Smith. Muffled squeak of loose floorboards inside the house drifted our way.

After more silence than I'd expected, one of the brutes inside yelled, "You badge-totin' sons of bitches can go straight to Hell, every damned one of you — however many that might actually be. And if'n yore really and truly who you say you be."

Second man called out, “You law-bringin’ idgits must think we’re all so stupid we’d have to study up to be a half-wit or somethin’. Ain’t none of us comin’ out.”

Another, deeper, voice chimed in with: “At ’eres fer damned sure. You ’uns could be any ole body out to rob and murder hymn-singin’, churchgoin’ folk like we’ens. You ’uns can come on in and take us, if’n you’ve got bark enough on yore dumb asses to try it. Otherwise, you can take them warrants, fold ’em four ways, and stick ’em where the sun don’t never shine.”

Couldn’t have been more than ten seconds later when both the windows, on either side of the cabin’s front door, erupted in a withering wall of rifle and pistol fire directed right at our water trough hidey-hole. Initial blasting sounded like someone was beating on the thick tank boards with hammers.

Billy rolled onto his back, scrunched down as low as he could get, and went to laughing. “Damnation, Hayden. Don’t know ’bout you, but I thought for sure that, given the chance, them evil sons of bitches would just stroll on out here like little girls goin’ to Sunday school and let us snap the irons on ’em. Just goes to show, you cain’t trust nobody nowadays.”

“You must have misjudged these particular

hard cases, my friend. Looks to me as though this bunch is determined to go down shooting."

Waves of screaming lead slapped the wooden trough, bored through the rough slats, sprayed water on us, and kicked up dirt all around both ends. Grass, where we'd crawled up from the hill, fell like wheat under one of Cyrus McCormick's mechanical harvesting machines.

Billy stared at his toes and yelled over the blasting, "Hope Carlton does something soon. Bunch of gun-crazed knot heads keeps pourin' lead on us at this pace, and they'll chew our wood-and-water hideout to pieces."

By and by, we smelled whiffs of smoke that got real heavy in pretty short order. Didn't take but a minute, or so, before we also detected random blasting from above and behind the shack. Carlton rained fire and lead on those killers' poorly built, one-plank roof like a springtime thundercloud. No other way to look at it. He made life mighty damned hot for those ole boys inside.

Storm of blue whistlers whizzing around me and Billy let up soon as we smelled the smoke. Silly chuckleheads, who'd been making our lives miserable, went to yelping and hollering like someone was chasing them around with hot branding irons. Couldn't have been more than five minutes later when the sun-bleached roof sprouted flames in several different places. Heavy clouds of greasy black smoke from pine pitch billowed out of the windows on either side of the rough-built cabin.

I glanced over at Billy. He grinned, sat up, and said, "Ain't no point layin' around here like we're on government salary or somethin'. Let's go get 'em, Hayden."

Before I could stop him, he jumped from behind our splintered, hole-filled cover, and started running for the front door like I'd seen him do at least a dozen times before. Really didn't matter that gunfire pointed our direction had pretty much stopped. He would have done the same thing even if those three killers were still pouring lead on us like rainwater from a boot.

Rail-thin deputy hit the first step on the wobbly porch and blew the door to smithereens in a shower of dust and splinters with blasts from both barrels of his ten-gauge boomer. Then he dropped the shotgun on the ground and hauled out those long-barreled Schofield .45s he favored. Sent five or six quick ones into the gravelike open space left by his assault. So much black powder smoke rolled toward the shuddering building's fractured doorway, you could barely see the front of the place by the time he let up for a second.

I was right on his heels when he stepped aside, smiled, and yelled, "Blister 'em with another round of hot lead, Hayden. Hit 'em with both barrels of that big blaster."

Jerked both triggers at the same time and sent buckshot into the walls on either side of the door. Each blast punched a window-sized hole. More heavy smoke almost blotted out any view of the doors and windows.

We could hear the men inside hooting, hollering, bouncing off the walls, and running around like chickens with their heads cut off. I pitched the shotgun aside and pulled my pistols as well, but before we could get indoors, I heard wood and glass splinter on the side of the building closest to the corral.

"Keep an eye peeled here, Billy. But stay outside, you hear. Don't want to confuse you with one of these killers. I'll go around, see who's trying to get away."

Turned the corner just in time to watch Buck Crowder dive through the shattered opening and land in the dirt, head first. He landed with a resounding thump beside a chair he'd thrown out ahead of his leap. All the clothing along his back, from his neck to his ankles, smoked and suddenly burst into flame, about a second after he hit the ground.

Crowder went to yelping, jumped up, and ran past me like a fully stoked locomotive. Poor bastard was slapping at his sides. Unfortunately, he couldn't reach his back, and made noises like a lunch whistle at a sawmill. By the time ole Buck got past me and headed around front for the creek, he looked like a pine-knot torch that had grown legs.

Since the burning outlaw had dropped all his weapons, and was considerably more concerned with putting the flames consuming his clothing out, figured I might as well direct my efforts elsewhere. Carlton ran up beside me, about then. He grinned from ear to ear and looked right pleased with himself.

"How'd you like my little campfire, Hayden?" he yelled.

"Mighty fine, Carl. You saved mine and Billy's bacon, for sure."

"Where is Billy?"

"Should be around front, near the door. You managed to set Buck Crowder on fire. He came foggin' out that window yonder, threw his weapons aside, and headed for the creek."

"Good. Got any idea where them other two are?"

"Unless they've managed to get out on the far side, guess they're still in with all the smoke and flame."

We hustled back to the front just in time to watch Billy disarm Coyle and Hillhouse. He grinned when we walked up and said, "They crawled out. Not much fight left in 'em, Hayden. Pitched most of their weapons on the porch and came to me on their hands and knees, like babies. Course they each had several hideout pistols on 'em that I had to take as well."

I said, "Let's get 'em up. Move 'em over there into the shade of that cottonwood. Away from this fire. Not gonna be anything left of the cabin in a few more minutes."

Coyle moaned and complained like an old woman when we made him stand and walk without help. He hobbled on his bad leg, griped, whined, and grumbled until he had covered the approximately forty feet and could sit again.

Hillhouse followed the poor stupid goober he'd shot less than an hour earlier and didn't say a word. But, my Lord Above, if the looks he threw our direction could have killed deputy U.S. marshals, all three of us would have been deader than hell in a

Baptist preacher's front parlor.

Carlton herded a burnt-blackened and soaking-wet Buck Crowder over to the prayer meeting. Amazing that ole Buck looked a lot worse off than he really was. Goodly amount of his clothing had suffered from the fire, and large splotches of hair had gone missing from his beard and head. Man had all the appearance of a stray dog that'd been put to flame, and then beat out with a broom.

Crowder flopped down beside his friends and said, "You didn't have to set me on fire, goddammit. Hadn't been for the creek bein' so close, like it were, I'd of plumb burnt up. But, hell, typical behavior a man has to expect from Parker's boys. Just out for a day of harassin' law-abidin' folk. Settin' poor cowboys like me afire for the bald-faced fun of it."

Carlton almost fell down laughing. "My God, Buck, but you always have had a talent for lyin' like a yeller dog. You ain't been a law-abidin' cowboy since some years before you turned thirteen. Been in trouble, of one kind or another, with the law ever since you knifed your pa through the gizzard up in the Wolf River country. And you're how old now? Thirty-five, forty? Makes you somethin' more'n a twenty-year career criminal."

Mo Coyle had evidently left any sense of humor he ever had in the dirt where Hillhouse shot him. He went to whining about his leg wound hurting at first. When that didn't get him any sympathy, he took a different track.

"What the hell you do-right boys want with us anyway? We ain't done nothing, lately."

Billy dropped the last new shell in his pistol and snapped it shut. "You're a lyin' pig, Mo. You and Buck was with Maynard Dawson and Charlie Storms, not too long ago, when they went on a killing rip that took almost a dozen lives. Gonna drag you boys back to Judge Parker. Let him hang the hell out of you."

For the first time, Selby Hillhouse spoke up. He had a low, quiet, sinister way of talking that made chill bumps run up and down a man's spine. "Wait just a damned minute here. Whatever problem you lawdogs have with these boys don't include me. I ain't had nothin' to do with any killings you're wantin' to lay on them. Wasn't nowhere near Boiling Springs."

Carlton winked at me and said, "Don't recall as how anybody mentioned Boiling Springs, Selby."

Hillhouse shot an angry, haggard look at Carlton. "I done heard all about it. Bunch of you law-bringin' fellers went out on a manhunt and got shot to pieces in a well-laid trap. That warn't good enough for you, so you went back again, and the same bunch done it to you twice."

"At least you got that part right. I'm one of those what got shot in the first ambush," Carlton said.

The beaten, fuming outlaw grinned and continued with: "Even hear tell as how *somebody* kilt Hamish Armstrong. Must've been one hell of a fight. Have to admit I liked Hamish. Only one of you badge-wearin' bastards what was worth a tinker's damn. But, still and all, you cain't place me within a hundred miles of either of those dustups. Didn't have nothin' to do with Armstrong's death, or shootin' any of you other boys."

Billy holstered his pistol, pulled a John Doe warrant and a stubby pencil from his vest pocket, and scratched a name on the blank line. He held the document up where Hillhouse could see it and said, "While that bilge you just rattled off might well be true, Selby, I know for a fact that you did murder a poor unarmed cowboy from south Texas named Del Cain down on the Muddy

Boggy. Shot the man for his saddle, a pair of boots, and three hundred dollars he'd earned on a cattle drive to Dodge. There's papers posted on you for that killin', and this John Doe covers you like a wet blanket."

When it comes to bad men, I've learned a number of hard, but simple, lessons during my years as a manhunter and assassin. One of the most important is that you should never, and I mean never, trust a bad man any farther than you can throw a fully loaded stagecoach.

Second thing I learned, through hard times on the track, is that once you've got evil scum under the gun, you should never get too close to one of them, until after they're shackled and chained, or, preferably, dead. Proximity might allow your captive to reach out and grab you. Just can't tell what in the way of awful results may occur after that.

A mistake in either instance could well mean the difference between life and death. But good men make mistakes — even men of Billy Bird's vast and varied experience.

Lanky marshal stepped over to within arm's length of Selby Hillhouse and waved the John Doe warrant under the killer's nose. "This piece of paper is gonna put you on the gallows, Selby," Billy said. "We're gonna watch you swing on Maledon's deadly play toy, down in the hollow from Judge Parker's courthouse."

True, his behavior bordered on the bold. Some might even say it was little more than an arrogant taunt. But the result of his mocking gibe never should have occurred.

The bad-tempered Hillhouse, who was responsible for at least a dozen killings, got a stricken look on his surly face. He leveled a quivering finger in Billy's face. "Ain't nobody gonna hang me, you bony-assed son of a bitch," he growled, and then jumped to his feet in a crouch.

As if by magic, one of those bone-handled Arkansas toothpicks appeared in his right hand. The knife flashed up and sidewise in his fist. Six inches of cold steel disappeared into Billy Bird's left side.

It's a mite easier, and quicker, to kill a man with a knife, up close, than it is for him to get firearms out for the work of defending himself. Had my pistols up instantly, but it was too late. God had already been there and left.

11
"You're Gonna Die Right Where You're Standing."

Billy let out a low, moaning grunt. The folded warrant slipped from his fingers and he watched, unbelieving, as it fluttered to the ground like a dying dove. My friend turned slowly toward me. A stricken, bewildered look passed over his face. He glanced down at the hole in his shirt, stumbled two or three steps my direction, and went to his knees as a frothy stream of bright, red blood bubbled from the gash. A shaking hand shot to the wound, as he tried to stanch the crimson flow. Dripping fingers clutched at the side of his bib-front shirt, but he couldn't stop what appeared as a river of gore.

"Damn, Hayden. This son of a bitch done went and stabbed me," he said weakly, then collapsed in a heap like a felled tree.

Carlton, pistol in hand to cover Hillhouse, darted over to our wounded friend's side, grabbed him by the arm, and dragged him away from any more harm.

Couldn't have taken more than five seconds before Cecil said, "Sweet Jesus, Hayden. Billy's hurt bad. The son of a bitch put that blade through a lung. Maybe even punched a hole in his heart." Then he turned on Hillhouse. "If he dies, I'll kill you myself, you murderin' son of a bitch."

An overpowering, but controlled, rage, the likes of which I'd never felt in my entire life, swept over me. Not even witnessing the death of Handsome Harry Tate, or the kidnapping of Elizabeth, had resulted in such anger. Unparalleled fury, tinged with murderous venom, rushed up from the soles of my feet, wrapped itself around my own icy heart in a viselike grip, and forced hot blood to my neck and face. Of a sudden, it felt as though the fires of a sulfurous, imp-infested hell lapped at the collar of my shirt.

Selby Hillhouse instantly recognized murder in my eyes as soon as he glanced my direction. He looked like a caged animal, as I waved my pistols at him.

Should never have hesitated. Should have killed him the instant the knife first appeared in his hand. Cannot, to this very day, justify in my own mind why I didn't. And trust me when I say, I've wept many times over the years for that deadly moment of indecision.

Only reason I've ever been able to come up with for such uncertainty involves the kind of behavior you can observe when big cats, like General Black Jack Pershing, catch a fat mouse. They love to play with their prey, before they kill and eat it.

Hillhouse took on the aspect of a man who'd just got religion. He pitched the knife on the ground and spit at the spot where Billy fell. His gaze darted from me to Carlton and back again.

Not a sign of regret in the heartless killer's voice when he said, "Given any chance a-tall, you should've known that I'm gonna kill all you Parker boys before you can get me back to Fort Smith."

Pretty sure my voice dropped so low he could barely hear me. Must have sounded like cold steel sliding across a frozen pond in January when I said, "You're not going back to Fort Smith, you stinkin' stack of human dung. In fact, you're not going one step off the spot where you are right this very moment."

Couldn't believe my eyes. I'd seen some nervy behavior from men like Hillhouse over the years, but his took the cake. The sorry blackguard actually had the brassy gall to pull tobacco from his vest pocket and start rolling himself a smoke.

"You cain't do nothin' about what just happened, lawdog. Cain't do a single, solitary thing, but take me back to Fort Smith for trial. Hell, Tilden, way I've got it figured, neither one of you boys is gonna make it that far. Bet both of you bite the dust along the trail somewheres."

"Oh, you're dead wrong about that, Selby," I said. "You're gonna cash in your chips right where you're standing. Even if you could bring back time, like God Almighty, and make it right, I'd still kill you. And if I didn't, trust me, Marshal Carlton J. Cecil would."

He threw his head back and laughed. Cackled like one of Satan's puss-covered demons. Put the smoke between his lips and struck a match. "Bullshit," he said, and put flame to the tobacco and started to light up.

The burning match still dangled from his fingers when I shot him once between the eyes and again in the heart, at the same instant. His hat flew off and a good-sized glob of brain matter splattered all over the trunk of the tree behind him, along with chunks of bone, lung, and heart. Blood sprayed his sorry friends, who gaped, wide-eyed, on the ground nearby.

Coyle and Crowder went to screaming

and rolled on their bellies like moles trying to dig in for the winter. A look of total surprise flickered over Hillhouse's pock-marked face as he went over backward like a felled tree and landed on a web of enormous cottonwood roots running along the top of the ground. I marched over to the motionless body, took careful aim, and shot him two more times.

Toed the corpse and said, "Say hello to Satan for me, you murdering son of a bitch. I'm sure he's got a place especially picked out for you." Turned to Cecil and said, "How's he doin', Carl?"

"He ain't good, Hayden. Jesus, I cain't get the bleedin' stopped."

The seething rage I felt had abated not one iota. Cocked both pistols and stomped my way to a cowering Buck Crowder. I figured him for the stronger of the two remaining murderers. Kicked the groveling slug in the side, and rolled him onto his back.

Leveled the barrel of one of my weapons up less than a foot from his head and said, "Stand up and die like a man, you back-shootin' skunk."

He threw shaking hands up in front of his face and squealed like a tortured child. "Please, oh, God, please don't shoot me!

Please don't do it! I didn't stab your friend."

"No, but you were there when rancher Tom Black got rubbed out. You contributed to the destruction of the entire Wilson family. Helped murder Jonas Two Hatchets and his wife. And you were there when Hamish Armstrong and Samuel Crazy Snake got shot to pieces just trying to do a thankless, dangerous job."

Crowder popped up on his knees and slapped his hands together like a man praying at a traveling tent revival. Tears streaked his soot-encrusted cheeks as he whimpered, "Not me. I swear it. It was them others. Me and Mo didn't kill nobody. We was there when them things happened, ain't no doubt 'bout that, Marshal. But I swear 'fore Jesus, neither of us took part in the raping, crucifying, or killing."

Behind me Carlton groaned, then shouted, "Billy Bird's dead, you sorry bastard."

Before I could even turn Carl's direction, Crowder's head exploded like a ripe watermelon. The huge bullet went in one side of his stupid noggin and blasted out the other in a saddle-sized spray of crimson gore, greasy hair, and bone. His limp body crumpled into a heap, the hands still extended in prayer.

Carlton darted past me, grabbed Coyle by the throat, and forced the still-smoking pistol's barrel into the screaming man's mouth. "You've got exactly five seconds, maggot. Where'd Dawson, Storms, and Rix go?" Then he started ticking off the quickly fleeting measure left in Mo Coyle's worthless life.

At the count of three, Coyle mumbled something around the pistol barrel I couldn't understand. Black powder smoke oozed out his mouth and nose with the words.

"For Christ's sake, Carl, let him talk," I said. "I can't figure out what he's saying with your gun in there."

Cecil jerked the weapon from of the outlaw's maw so abruptly, several teeth came out along with it. Coyle grabbed his spurting mouth and yelped like a shot dog.

"Swhit a'mighty. You bwoke my tweeth out. Gwad damn."

My red-haired, red-faced partner pressed the muzzle of his shooter against Coyle's temple till the man's eyes crossed. Carlton was nigh to screaming when he said, "Where'd they go, damn you? I'm not gonna ask again."

"Twexas. Twhey went to Twexas. Gonna mweet up wid Rwufus Dwoome." He fingered the newly excavated hole in his mouth and spit pieces of his broken teeth onto the ground.

Carlton leaned down, put his lips next to Coyle's ear, and yelled so loud dead folks buried in Fort Smith must have heard him. "It's a damned big state, Coyle. Where 'bouts in Texas, you son of a bitch?"

Coyle hacked and spit until he finally got control of his damaged, rubbery lips again. "We split up after the fracas at Boiling Springs. Maynard said if Hayden Tilden caught up with us, no one would come out of it alive." Tears streamed down the man's cheeks.

"Leastways, you dumb bastards got one thing right," Carlton snarled.

Coyle flinched like he'd been slapped, but then went on with his tale. "Well, anyway, Charlie and Cotton decided to head south for Hell's Half Acre in Fort Worth. Said they was plenty of whores, liquor, and gamblin' available to men of the world. Figured they could get lost amongst all them passin' cowboys on their way to the railheads. And besides, Rufus and Jethro Doome was already in residence and could maybe see to helping them hide out."

"By God, Carlton," I said, "I can't wait to put a bullet, or three, in Rufus Doome. How long you reckon it'll take us to get from here to Fort Worth?"

"Week. Maybe ten days. Depending on how hard you want to travel."

I glanced over at the lifeless body of my good friend Billy Bird. "We'll put this piece of trash to diggin' holes, right now. Get Billy in the ground, and then we'll head out — maybe tomorrow afternoon or early the next morning."

Carlton glared at Coyle and snapped, "What about this son of a bitch? We gonna kill him, or what?"

Shattered, bloody-mouthed gunman looked like a caged rat. "Oh, please, God. I done told you what you wanted to know. You wouldn't kill me now. Would you?"

I made a hasty assessment of our situation, and an even hastier decision on Coyle's immediate future. "We'll take him with us. If we run across any of Judge Parker's other deputy marshals out here, before we reach the Red River, we'll send him along to Fort Smith with them. If not, he might well be of some help in finding Dawson and the others once we reach Fort Worth. Right now, he's gonna dig three graves — two over in the weeds by the water trough and one right here under this cottonwood."

Carlton nodded, and stared at our dead

friend. And then, as if to himself, he said, "Damnation. Guess Billy ain't never gonna get to see Moonlight Two Hatchets again."

Took Coyle all that afternoon, and most of the next day, to dig those graves, in spite of the softness of the rich red soil. Carlton kept after him pretty hot and heavy to get them done as quickly as he could. Course Coyle griped, whined, procrastinated, and complained about being made to do the job alone. All the bad-tempered grumping stopped after Carl put the barrel of his shotgun to the outlaw's temple and asked if he'd rather be dead and buried with the others.

"I can most assuredly arrange it," Carl growled.

We put Hillhouse and Crowder in the ground first. Then turned our attention to our good friend. Wrapped him in a favorite blanket he'd always carried for cold nights, along with most of the leaves from a big sage bush — just so he'd smell good a little longer. I took his Schofield pistols and gave them to Carl. Tears etched hard lines on his dusty cheeks as he accepted those beautiful weapons.

"I know he wouldn't want them in the ground all rusted up and turning into junk, Carl. Man loved 'em way too much for such an ending," I said. "Handsome Harry left his Colts to me. I'm sure Billy would want you to have these."

Stood beside Billy's finished, dirt-covered grave and, for the first time since I'd started working for Judge Parker, I felt at a total loss for words. For a spell there, I couldn't think of anything in the way of fine-sounding passages from Shakespeare, or the Bible, to read over a man I loved like a brother. Sending him off with second-hand words just didn't seem appropriate. Deep down in the secret recesses of my own heart, I just felt he deserved something a lot more personal.

Glanced over at Carl. He swayed slowly from foot to foot like a weeping willow in a hot breeze and twisted his hat in his hands. Poor man's face was still damp with tears. Sounded on the verge of completely breaking down when he said, "Ain't no point in looking to me, Hayden. Scarcely know what to think right now. Me and Billy done rode together for years. Fought many a bad man. No matter how stiff our competition, he always came out of every fight with nary a scratch. Sweet Jesus, I never thought it'd come to this — stabbed to death." He slapped his leg with his hat. A quivering chin dropped onto his chest. "Dammit, I just cain't believe it, and cain't talk no more — not right now."

Took some doing, but I finally choked back the leaking from my own eyes and mustered up enough gumption to make my friend's entrance into God's blue heaven as smooth as possible. Not since Handsome Harry's death at the hands of Brutus Sneed had I been so overcome with emotion.

Held my hat over my heart, gazed past cotton-boll clouds, and wept like a child as I said, "Well, Lord, you know Billy Bird. He'd been the pointed instrument of your retribution for many a long year before I met him. Altogether, I suppose, Billy must have fought in over a hundred bloody encounters with bad men of every sort. He brought that many killers and thieves to justice for their infamous deeds. A body couldn't ask for a better companion, out here in the big cold and lonely. He never complained — no matter how bad a situation we managed to find ourselves in. He always led the way into trouble, and saved my life, and Carl's, more times than either of us care to remember. We're both alive today because of this man. Me and Carlton, and a host of others, will sorely miss his smiling presence. He was as pleasant a fellow as I've ever had the good fortune to know — absolutely the finest sort in his native humor and conduct."

Of a sudden, I couldn't go on. Took a second to recover myself. Bent down and scooped up a pile of dirt from my friend's grave. From somewhere so far back in my memory I couldn't bring out exactly how or when, I dredged up the pieces of a passage a preacher used during a funeral service I'd attended as a boy.

Pretty sure I scrambled the prayer some when I said, "In the midst of all life, death is forever with us. Now, in the sure and certain belief in the Resurrection and Eternal Life, we commit our friend to the ground. Ashes to ashes, earth to earth, dust to dust. All glory be to the Father, and the Son, and the Holy Spirit. Amen."

Heard Carlton whisper, "My God, he's gone. Billy, my good friend. My dear God."

We covered Billy Bird's final resting place with all the water-smoothed stones from Wild Cat Creek we could locate. Put up a marker Carl fashioned from a plank he pulled out of what was left of the cabin's remaining wall. He even built a red-hot fire, heated up a piece of iron, and burned Billy's name into the heavily weathered board, along with a heartfelt message. Took him a spell of nasty work, but the final effort turned out right impressive. Brought more tears when we stood back and read it.

HERE LIETH
WILLIAM TECUMSEH BIRD
HE FOUGHT FOR THE RIGHT — A BANE
TO THE WICKED
A FINE FRIEND

Some years later, I happened to be on Pine Mountain again. As I remember it now, that was the time I went out looking for a murderous skunk named Bergan Muscleshell. Muscleshell was the whiskey-peddlin' scum who shot Deputy Marshal Clyde Koontz in the back, up in the Arbuckle Mountains. Koontz, and the way he died, kind of reminded me of Billy. Guess maybe that's what caused me to get to wondering about my old friend. Anyway, I took the time and stopped for a spell at Wild Cat Creek just to check on him.

His grave appeared to have been well kept and was undisturbed after all that time — except for one significant difference. Someone had replaced our handmade wooden cross with a large, beautifully polished, carefully inscribed piece of Arkansas granite.

Carlton always denied responsibility. Said he was absolutely certain Moonlight Two

Hatchets did it. Such sentiment proved way too much for me to deny. So I just left it alone. Always felt Billy would've been pleased to know a beautiful woman still cared enough about him, long years after he'd passed, to do such a thing.

12
"Said He'd Kill Me Deader'n a Brass Spittoon . . ."

We spurred our animals away from the horrors of Pine Mountain and struck out across the rolling grasslands. Over the years, it's been my experience that most times the best thing to do, when it comes to death, is simply ride away from it as quickly as possible. People who sit around and dwell on God's great plan can drive themselves to distraction. The madhouses used to fill up with such folks every spring.

Can't say as how our actions mattered much, though. Carlton and I were both steeped in a depressing melancholy funk we couldn't shake off. Felt for all the world like a heavy, black cloud had come over us. The fog of sorrow that engulfed our hearts just wouldn't be burned away by the sunlight of gratitude we should have felt for having been spared and still able to count our own selves among the living.

We took a ferry across the Muddy Boggy

near Atoka, and headed for Tishomingo, capital of the Chickasaw Nation. Carlton allowed as how he couldn't stand the sight of Mo Coyle any longer. I had intended on killing every member of Dawson's bunch. Can't really say to this day why I let Coyle live. My angry friend commented that, every time he looked at the sorry sack of dung, it reminded him of Billy Bird's foul murder, and how much he itched to put a bullet in Coyle's head.

Carlton figured it best we get shed of the outlaw, quick as we could. And being as how them Chickasaws had such a fine, sturdy, brick courthouse and jail, we could dump him off with the Indian police in Tishomingo, and go on our way to Fort Worth and Hell's Half Acre. Sounded like a good plan to me, so that's what we did.

But as we dragged Coyle off his horse and pushed him toward them Chickasaw folks' well-built brick building, and the certainty of a spell behind bars before being shipped off to Fort Smith and hanged, we bumped into Deputy Marshal Heck Taylor.

Heck strolled from the front door of the courthouse and grabbed me by the hand. A robust, vigorous man who appeared to have never met a skillet full of eggs or slab of bacon he didn't like, he sported an outsized handlebar mustache and a friendly, jovial disposition. Those traits tended to belie a deadly adversary when hot lead started flying his direction.

We shook and he said, "What you got here, Tilden? Looks like the one and only Morton Coyle, to me."

"That's the man, Heck. We caught him up near Wild Cat Creek on Pine Mountain in the company of other killers just as bad — or worse. Had to shoot hell out of a couple of them — Buck Crowder and Selby Hillhouse."

Taylor's blue-eyed gaze flicked from Carlton to Coyle to me before he said, "My sweet Lord. You boys done went and killed Selby Hillhouse?"

Carlton grunted and said, "Deader'n a rotten willow stump. But it came at a mighty dear cost. Sorry son of Satan stabbed Billy Bird to death, 'fore we could stop it."

"Oh, my God. You don't mean it? Killed Marshal Billy Bird, did he? Well, that Hillhouse feller was a bad 'un. And to tell the righteous truth, I've got a warrant for him right here in my vest pocket."

"What's it for?" I asked.

"He murdered a traveling dentist from over near Van Buren. Caught the defenseless tooth-puller about ten miles outside Vinita. Shot the man for four dollars and a horse. Had hoped to bring the murderin' skunk in myself, but if you've put him in the ground, that's just as good."

Carl said, "Tell you what we'll do, Heck. Bein' as how Hayden done went and snatched a bit of change from your pocket by rubbing out Hillhouse, we'll let you have this insect as a replacement." He pushed Coyle toward Taylor. "All you have to do is take him back to Arkansas and collect whatever you can get on him. We've gotta make a quick trip to Fort Worth. Have information that the Dawson bunch is hiding out in Hell's Half Acre."

"One condition, though," I added.

The full-bodied marshal muscled Coyle into a chair sitting beside the courthouse door, grinned, and said, "Figured there had to be a catch. And what would that be, Marshal Tilden?"

"Do you have any posse men along with you on this trip?"

"Why, yes, I do as a matter of plain fact. Nate Swords. Fine feller. Better at coverin' my back than any man I've ever rode with. Trust him with my life."

"We'll trade you Coyle for Swords," I said. "Need at least one more gunhand along with us for this trip. Actually, could use two or three, but we'll settle for Swords."

Taylor's gaze darted over my shoulder. He raised a beefy hand and pointed. "Well, here he comes now. Monetary proposition you've presented sounds fine to me. But you'll have to talk with Nate 'bout goin' to Texas. I cain't be makin' such decisions for the man."

Nate Swords looked more than capable. And, after the shock of erroneous recognition, I had to admit that he reminded me more than a bit of Billy Bird. Tall and lanky, his shoulder-length hair sprouted from under a military style campaign hat, spilled over the collar of a fringed leather shirt, and matched the strawlike color of a droopy mustache. He sported case-hardened Colt's pistols in the butts-forward, Wild Bill Hickok fashion, and appeared totally comfortable in well-used canvas pants and soft knee-high cavalry officer's boots. Entire getup was highlighted with a pair of the most ornate Mexican spurs I'd seen since Lucius Dodge went out with me and Carlton to kill Martin Luther Big Eagle, up in Red Rock Canyon.

Marshal Taylor took the situation in hand as Swords ambled up beside him. Placed a brawny arm around his posse man's shoulders and said, "Nate, this here is Hayden Tilden and his good friend Deputy Marshal Carlton J. Cecil. These boys are on their way to Fort Worth. Have reliable information that Maynard Dawson is holed up in Hell's Half Acre. Hayden was a-wonderin' if'n you'd like to tag along. Be mighty good experience for you, if'n you should be interested in my particular opinion."

A toothy grin spread over Swords's face, as he extended his hand my direction. "Damned sure would. Be my privilege to ride along with you, Marshal Tilden. Been hearin' about the exploits of you and Marshal Cecil for some time now. A pleasure to make your acquaintance."

"Well, then," I said as we shook hands, "it's settled. We'll leave at first light tomorrow morning. Want to try and catch up with Dawson and Storms before they hightail it for New Mexico, Arizona, or points even farther west."

Later that afternoon, I sent a telegraph message to Fort Smith that informed the U.S. marshal and Judge Parker of Billy's unfortunate demise. Might well have been the most difficult missive I'd ever had to write, up to that point in my life. Also penned a heartfelt note of regret to my long-suffering wife. Apologized for not being at home with her, and threw everything into that note I could think of to ease the pain of having to be away in the wilds of godforsaken Texas for the good Lord only know show long.

Nate Swords turned out to be a real blessing. His cheerful demeanor, boundless good humor, and joking manner did wonders toward livening mine and Carlton's damaged spirits. Memories of Billy Bird's unfortunate passing slowly faded to the backs of our troubled minds, over the next few days, thanks to Nate.

By the time we ran upon Deputy Marshal Caleb Masters, about ten miles north of the Red River, we'd healed plenty enough for another dustup with some of the Indian Territories' most vicious criminal element. Caleb Masters was just the man to provide such a distraction.

We found the famed marshal, near day's end, camped under a sheltering oak. He'd cooked coffee, and we could smell it long before Carlton spotted him. Eased up on the man so as not to surprise him, but he'd already taken note of our approach through his long glass, and readily invited us to step down and take our leave.

Carlton, who'd known Marshal Masters for some years, appeared extremely pleased with the chance meeting. He hopped off his animal and grabbed the tall, black lawman's hand. Then, he turned to me and our new helper and said, "Caleb, not sure you know my friends. This here's Hayden Tilden and our new posse man, Nate Swords."

Masters offered everyone a toothy grin, nodded, and waved his acceptance of our presence. Then, he motioned for us to unsaddle our mounts, sit, and partake of his welcoming campfire.

In a deep, rumbling voice, tinged with the molasseslike undertones of Mississippi, or Alabama, our host said, "Glad to see you fellers. Don't know what you're doin' way out here, but you're welcome to the fire and the stump juice. I could sure use some assistance shortly, if'n you've a mind, and the time, to give it." The marshal reminded me of a somewhat smaller version of Judge Parker's famed deputy Barnes Reed, who'd accompanied Carlton and me on our Red Rock Canyon raid.

We unburdened our horses and threw our traps on the ground near his smoldering campfire. I poured a full cup from Marshal Masters's soot-covered coffeepot. Blew on and sipped at the kind of belly wash that'd grow hair on a saddle. Said, "Well, we should be able to help you out, Caleb, as long as our stay doesn't last more'n a day or two."

Masters smiled again. "You boys arrived at just the best possible instant. Late tomorrow, or maybe the next mornin', 'bout ten miles south of here, at the Delaware Bend Crossing on the Red, Tom Dozier's gonna push a small herd of stolen horses back into the Nations from Texas. I intend to catch him in the act and put an end to his thievin' ways, for once and all."

Carlton perked up. "That a fact, now? Tom Dozier for absolute certain, Caleb? Hell, that sorry rascal's been stealin' and killin' all over the countryside for as long as I've been carryin' a badge for Judge Parker. And if my sometimes addled memory serves, you've been after him, off and on, that whole time."

Masters served up a weak grin. "Well, he's one sly, sneakin' son of a bitch, and has managed to stay about half a step ahead of me through the efforts of his friends and confederates in crime. They've displayed an uncanny ability, over the years, to warn him of my presence, on a number of occasions when I truly thought I had him dead to rights. I can assure you boys, the whole of my experience with the man has been most frustratin'."

"Well, now, guess we all know as how bad folks here in the Nations are inclined to assist the outlaw element in their nefarious endeavors. At times, it does seem there's a lookout posted on every hill," I offered.

Nate perked up and said, "Ain't Dozier the feller what likes to leave notes warnin' that he'll by-God kill the hell out of anyone doggin' his trail?"

Me and Carlton had heard such stories as well. Way most folks told them, Dozier maintained a particularly large and knotty twist in his trapdoor drawers about Caleb Masters in particular, and never missed an opportunity to taunt the man. Carl and me would never have broached that particular subject. Came as something of a surprise that Nate brought it up. Have to admit, I was somewhat taken aback that Caleb didn't seem to mind the subject in the least.

"Yes, well, the sorry scoundrel's left notes for me all over the countryside after he robbed stores, banks, cattle buyers, stagecoaches, and even a poker game or two. Said he'd kill me deader'n a brass spittoon in a Denver whorehouse, if'n I didn't stop a-followin' him."

Carlton pitched what was left of his cup of up-and-at-'em juice into the fire and said, "Reckon he meant it, Caleb?"

Masters sat up, fetched out tobacco and makin's, and began rolling himself a smoke. "Oh, he's killed many a time before. Well known in some circles for his lethal behavior. Have no doubt he'd do it again, if given a choice between that and spending a few years in the Detroit Correctional Facility." He licked the paper on his hand-rolled cigarette, as big around as my finger, lit it, and went to making smoke like a fire built from wet wood.

"How long have you been after him this time out?" I asked.

"More'n two weeks. Came upon what I feel is some mighty good information when I dropped a couple of prisoners off in Tuskahoma for safekeeping. After years of close calls and fruitless chases, pretty sure this 'uns gonna end in success. Have a good feelin' 'bout it."

The conversation kind of dwindled off, after that. Carlton, Nate, and me were bone tired and ready for a restful night's sleep. Darkness and dreams came down on my head like an anvil dropped from Heaven's front gate.

I must not have even stirred through the whole night. Next morning, I woke up lying in the same position that I'd snoozed off in. Every bone in my body ached like someone had whipped me all night long with a barrel stave.

We broke camp about sunup, and an hour later picketed our animals and pitched another camp in a stand of weeping willow trees, fifty or sixty yards west of Delaware Bend Crossing. Dragged up as much underbrush as we could find and placed it between our hideout and the river. Caleb noted that the added concealment couldn't hurt our cause.

Nate enjoyed himself immensely. He said, "This is like fortin' up when I was a little kid playin' Indians and cavalry back in Kentucky." Was the first time I noted something of the child that still occasionally presented itself in the man's personality.

We spent most of the rest of the day hunting and fishing along the river in both directions. Didn't kill anything, but caught a fine mess of pan-sized sunfish Carlton fried up that night. Nate turned out to be one hell of a fisherman. He caught most of them. It was a right funny experience to watch him. Man beamed with childish excitement every time he got a nibble. Relaxed mood of that single afternoon went a long way toward soothing the ache I still felt over Billy's sad passing.

Early the following morning, a feller riding

a dappled gray showed up on the Texas bank of the Red. Marshal Masters went out and motioned him to our side. Stranger waded across. Water only came up to about his animal's hocks and was barely flowing.

Caleb and the new arrival talked for a spell out of our earshot. After a few minutes, the unknown rider cast a nervous glance over his shoulder, pointed to where he'd just come from, and hurried off to the northeast at a trot.

Masters hustled back to where we'd hid ourselves in the trees. Called us together and said, "Sure you've figured it out by now, but at 'ere was my informant. He done brought me word as how Tom Dozier's definitely on his way."

Carlton scratched his stubble-covered chin. "How long 'fore he gets here?"

"Maybe an hour or so. Way my man told it, Dozier and two or three other thievin' snakes are a-leadin' a right nice herd of twelve to fifteen horses they stole from a rancher down near Gainesville. Must have been some shootin' in the process. Not for certain, but one of the bandits might already have some lead in him."

Nate levered a round into the chamber of his old Yellow Boy Winchester. "Well," he said, "guess we'd all best get hid somewheres, hadn't we? Wanna make sure we surprise these boys when they show up."

Caleb nodded his agreement. "Here's how I figured we'd play it, fellers. Me and Hayden'll stay mounted and brace 'em soon's they get about midstream. Trail from the river climbs up that steep wash, over yonder. There ain't much room to maneuver between the cut banks on either side of the wash. Pinched off the way it is, Dozier and his men should have to walk the herd up."

"Where you want me and Nate?" Carlton asked.

"You boys pick a spot. Hide along the ridge on either side of the cut. Want all of us to try and come out at 'em at the same time." He waved in the general direction of scrubby areas on the opposite crests of the wash. "We get 'em bottled up real good, and it should be easy to grab these fellers without much of a fight."

While that's the way Caleb figured on the thing, it'd been my experience bad men seldom wanted to cooperate when a lengthy stay behind bars in a stone-cold hard-rock Northern prison was most likely in their future. Yep, thieving, murdering, raping, horse-stealing bastards tended to fight for their sorry lives. And that kind of attitude usually proved especially true if such men found themselves in the company of other sons of bitches who'd willingly go down shooting, rather than spend time swinging a sledgehammer up in a desolate Michigan penitentiary.

Carlton slapped the butts of his pistols. He had the look in his frosty gray eyes of a man primed for a blood-letting, and itching to get at it. My friend never would have admitted it, but I'm sure he felt about the same way I did. It was time for some retribution, even if that meant killing two or three men who had absolutely nothing to do with Billy Bird's unfortunate death.

What we both craved, more than whiskey, women, or gold, was some much-needed release from our grief. Shooting the hell out of a couple of known killers sounded like a damned fine idea to me, whether Caleb saw it that way or not.

"Guess we'd best get set up. I'll take the east flank of the trail. Nate can take the west," Carlton said. Then, he turned to me. "Caleb's plan sounds like a good 'un. But just 'tween you and me, my friend, if these ole boys stampede their herd, there'll be hell to pay if we ain't on our toes. So, you cover his back, Hayden. That'll put two men in front of 'em, and one on each side. If them boys start their horses running, get to cover quick — cross fire from my direction could get downright murderous."

So, that's the way we worked it. Once Carlton and Nate got hid out and settled down in the scrub, Masters and me staked us out a shady spot under a friendly tree and tied our animals. Found us place to sit, piled up a mound of them big ole dead cottonwood leaves for comfort — and waited.

In spite of anything Caleb's informant might have thought, took a good bit more than an hour for those bad boys to show up. I kept checking my two-dollar Ingersoll pocket watch. The wait eventually turned into almost three hours. A blazing sun had got up pretty good, by then. Blistering heat, buzzing flies, and skeeters got right bothersome. I was in the process of trying to shoo one of those big, ugly, yellow jacket wasps out of my face when Caleb reached over, poked me on the leg, and pointed toward Texas.

"They're here," he whispered.

As we got ourselves horsed, half-a-dozen or so sleek-coated, well-fed hay burners eased up to the shallow river's ragged edge, and gazed at the far bank barely a hundred feet away. For a few fleeting seconds, those animals in the front rank hesitated, nervously pawed at the shallow water, but eventually waded in and started across.

A rider, who sported a brace of heavy, silver-plated pistols high on his waist, dressed in the short jacket and concho-decorated pants of a Mexican vaquero, trotted up. Horse thief didn't waste any time checking the river. Bold as brass, and with what appeared to be very little thought on the matter, he slapped a wide-brimmed sombrero against his leg, whistled, and urged the hesitant broncos down the muddy embankment.

Me and Caleb kicked over to a spot that should have served to block the herd's progress. Personally thought we'd moved a mite too soon, and had barely reined up when, under his breath, I heard Caleb mutter, "Damn the bad luck. Bastards always have brothers."

His odd declaration at such a charged moment got my attention right quick. "What is it?" I snapped. "What's the problem?"

In his excitement and duress, the black marshal's soft Southern accent shortened and became more clipped. "I recognize that horse-stealin' brush popper comin' over now. It's Dorsey Cobb, one of the most evil sons of bitches I ever knowed, or heard about."

"So?"

"Pert sure, if Dorsey's around, that means his brother Millard is probably back there in the herd somewheres. Problem is, Millard's worse than Dorsey ever thought about bein'. Separate and alone, either of them boys can be a handful. When you put the two of 'em in the company of a scoundrel like Tom Dozier, you're looking at a fierce, bloody gunfight, for sure."

Those prophetic words had barely escaped Caleb Master's lips when the man he'd just identified spotted the two of us. Dorsey Cobb had almost made it to our side of the river, by then. He pulled a long-barreled Remington pistol. Didn't hesitate for a second. Audacious thief set to punching holes in the air, all around us, with blue whistlers. Skittish horses bolted like God had jabbed them in the flanks with a flaming pitchfork.

Panicked herd surged out of the water at a dead run. Headed straight for me and Caleb. About then, a second and third bandit appeared on the far bank of the meandering Red. They pushed a like number of animals, and both launched into a rash of random, promiscuous blasting as soon as they realized that something they hadn't planned on, and didn't quite understand, had occurred.

The cut in the Nations' share of the riverbank funneled the charging hammerheads down to no more than three ponies abreast — just the way Caleb had expected. Only trouble was, those spooked, red-eyed broomtails were in a panic, as they hoofed their way up the rugged trail that led past us.

Caleb kicked his animal to Carlton's side of the cut and managed to get out of the stampede's way — just in the nick of time. I jerked Gunpowder in the opposite direction and spotted Nate Swords as he stood, leveled up his Winchester, and blasted Dorsey Cobb out of the saddle. All those ringtailed knot heads charged past me in sheer terror. Ahead of them, a whooping second rider snatched his pinto mount to a stiff-legged stop when he spotted his wounded comrade struggling in the mud.

Dorsey Cobb clutched at a hole in his bloody left side and scrambled to uncooperative feet, attached to shaky legs. Second outlaw twirled his mount in a tight circle and yelled, "Dorsey. Have the ambushin' bastards done went and kilt you, brother?"

Thief's concerned speechifying led me to believe the still-horsed brigand had to be Millard Cobb. He laid the spur on hard in what appeared an absolutely futile effort at helping his wounded brother in a time of desperate, life-threatening need. Poor stupid goober didn't make it far, though.

Carlton J. Cecil jumped from behind what was left of a lightning-slashed tree stump and shot the horse from under Cobb before it could take more'n half-a-dozen steps. Three thunderous, rapid-fire blasts from Carl's rifle, and the animal tipped over — end to end. Landed on top of, and damned near buried, its rider in the squishy embankment. The fallen and dazed Millard Cobb crawled from under the flopping animal, wobbled to his knees with a pistol in each hand. He fired blindly at everything in general and nothing in particular.

In all the confusion of whinnying horses, thundering hooves, flying mud, splashing water, gunfire, and spent black powder, the third thief had miraculously and totally disappeared from view. Guess everyone in our party must have zeroed in on Millard Cobb at about the same time. Like me, I suppose the others figured the already shot-to-hell Dorsey posed somewhat less of a threat than his dazed, but still-in-one-piece, brother. As it worked out, all four of us fired at almost the same instant, and riddled Millard Cobb with so many holes, my grandma could have used his perforated corpse as a flour sifter.

A stunned Dorsey turned just in time to see his bumbling brother flung sidewise by a death-dealing curtain of rifle and pistol bullets. The mortally wounded Millard staggered several steps and fired both his hand cannons into the muddy bog at his feet, before he collapsed into a bloody, lifeless heap.

Remaining of the Cobb brothers squealed like a baby pig caught under a gate. He struggled mightily to keep himself upright, turned back our direction, and sent more lead from a blazing weapon in each hand. Appeared to have put several shots into the fleeing herd, as he thrashed about in the mud.

'Bout then, I spotted Carlton out of the corner of my eye again. He stood in front of the scorched stump he'd used for cover. Shook his head like a man who was having trouble believing what his own eyes showed him. Couldn't have been more than a second's worth of decision making involved in what happened next. Carlton levered a shell into his Winchester, took careful aim, and sent Dorsey Cobb to Hell's front doorstep in a heartbeat with a well-placed shot to the thinker box. Bullet obliterated ole Dorsey's right eye and sent a gob of brain matter, bone, and blood as big as my fist squirting into the air behind him like a South American jungle parrot taking flight.

Poor skull-shot churn head, who didn't realize he was dead yet, snapped stiff in the knees, caved in at the chest, and went down like a rotted telegraph pole. Of a sudden, the confused and gory scene got quieter than daybreak on Easter Sunday. Got so peaceful I detected a soft breeze blowing across the river from Texas that whispered in the cottonwoods along the creek bank. Thought I could even hear the barely detectable, sluggish movement of the river.

Holstered one of my persuaders and reloaded the other, as Caleb spurred his horse up beside me and dismounted. I climbed off Gunpowder and, together, we surveyed the mess left behind by all the shouting, shooting, killing, and dying.

"Damn, Hayden," Caleb said. I detected the sound of deep regret in the man's voice. He slapped his reins against his leg. "Sure do hate that them three horses had to pay such a high price in this Pecos promenade."

"You can blame the unfortunate deaths of at least two of them on the Cobb brothers. You see where Dozier went?"

Masters snatched his hat off, made a sweeping gesture toward the Nations, and with considerable disgust in his voice said,

"Snaky son of a bitch slipped away from me again. Can't hardly believe it. Guess I'll have to spend some time sortin' out all these tracks till I find which way he went. Be on his sorry ass like prickly heat soon's we get these other fellers planted."

Carlton and Nate ambled up. Both men shoved fresh rounds into their rifles. Nate said, "Don't worry 'bout these boys, Caleb. Since I killed one, and all of us probably have a round in the other'n, we'll plant 'em. That is, if you want to go ahead and get on after Dozier, 'fore the slippery skunk puts too much distance between the two of you."

Masters slapped his hat back on his head, nodded like he agreed but was reluctant to leave, and jumped into the saddle. "I'm much obliged, fellers. Owe you one. Ever need another gun, be sure and look me up." He gave us a military-type farewell salute, and kicked north.

Carl shot a quick glance at the two bodies. "Sure do get tired of diggin' holes for worthless, no-account sons of bitches."

Nate grinned and flicked a bead of sweat from his brow. "The Nations is chocked full of sons of bitches, Carl. Personally, I'd a lot rather bury them, as have it the other way around."

"Well," I said, "let's get at it. We'll scratch

a couple of shallow graves out for these boys, quick as we can, and head south. Fort Worth and the Maynard Dawson bunch are waitin'. Real good chance the blood-letting we just witnessed ain't nothing compared to what's in store for us in Hell's Half Acre."

13
"I'm Gonna Whip You Like a Tied Yard Dog . . ."

Once you cross over into the great Lone Star State at Red River Station, when making your way out of the Nations, finding Fort Worth's pretty much a snap. Hadn't given it a great deal of thought till after we got into Texas pretty deep, but I'd never visited the busy cow town before and, as it turned out, neither had Carlton or Nate.

Just kept our horses pointed south on the pounded-to-dust old Chisholm Trail. At the river crossings, that famed passage usually measured a hundred to two hundred yards across, and in the countryside could easily spread out for more than a mile. Easy as it proved to follow, we still, somehow, managed to miss the bustling town by about two miles toward the east, anyway. But as soon as we hit the Texas and Pacific Railroad, and turned west, finding the rough cattle town was as easy as shooting fish in a rain barrel.

Arrived in front of the T & P Depot and headed north on Main Street. Carlton allowed as how if them Fort Worth folks named the dusty, horse-apple-littered thoroughfare *Main Street,* they must have had a good reason for it.

My parched trail mates quickly expressed a desire to stop and order up some liquid refreshment, being as how they'd spent so much time in the wilds without partaking.

Carlton said, "How 'bout a beaker of the old espiritus ferminti, Hayden? Sure could use somethin' to cut this lung-cloggin' Texas dust."

We passed on one joint with a sign out front that deemed it the Palace. Rough tavern didn't look much like any palace we'd ever seen. Finally decided to tie up and ask directions at a watering hole as crowded as a Baptist tent revival called the Emerald Saloon. Busy booze emporium was three blocks further up the heavily traveled street from the so-called Palace.

Main reason we stopped at that particular cow country oasis was because Nate spotted a sign out front touting the coldest beer in Fort Worth. Appeared to me the owners had opened the establishment as near the depot as possible in order to take advantage of arriving or departing travelers desperate for a drink.

Dismounted and carried our long guns with us. Guess we caused something of a stir. Strolled in all covered in trail dust, decorated with heavy silver badges, and bristling with all manner of weapons.

Cool, dark, and peaceful, the fancied-up cantina sported a solid mahogany bar that ran all the way across the far end of the room, and an impressive mirrored back bar. The Emerald turned out to be a right nice joint.

Smiling bartender sported an astonishing head of greased black hair, wore a garter on his sleeves, and looked like you could roller skate on him. He flashed a sparkling gold tooth at us and said, "Step right up, gents. Welcome to the Emerald. Name's Corky Tull. You fellers sure as hell don't look like cowboys."

Nate grinned as we bellied up to the spotless, highly polished bar and found a comfortable spot on the rail for our hot, booted feet. He said, "How can you tell we ain't cowboys, Corky?"

Whiskey slinger ran a finger under his waxed mustache. "Them badges yore wearin' is somethin' of a tell, as my gamblin' compadres would say. Besides, ain't ever seen no Texas waddies in the Emerald carryin' so many heavy gauge blasters at one time. Goodness gracious, fellers, just how many are you totin' there? I count at least three pistols and a rifle on each of you."

"Well, Corky, in our line of business it's always a good idea to be prepared," Carl said, as he propped his long guns against the bar.

I laid my .45-70 and Greener in front of me. Said, "That sign out front for real and true, Mr. Tull? You actually have ice-cold beer for sale in this stellar-looking concern?"

"Absolutely true statement of fact, sir." Corky Tull's grin got even bigger as he drew mugs of the coldest brew that ever tickled my parched tonsils. "First one's on the house, gents, and it's my pleasure to serve you," he said, as he refilled those quickly drained beakers. About a minute after our second round arrived, the three of us stood at Corky Tull's squeaky clean bar all smiles, with big foamy mustaches over our lips.

Our host wiped in front of me with a wet rag. "Thought you boys might be Texas Rangers, at first. But you ain't quite as rough-lookin' as most of the Rangers who come in here? So, I'm guessin' you ain't Rangers."

"No, sir," I said. "We're deputy U.S. marshals with the Western District Court of

Arkansas, His Honor Judge Isaac C. Parker presiding, out of Fort Smith."

He never stopped smiling. "Well, I'll just be certainly damned. You boys work for the famed Hanging Judge Parker. Kinda out of your normal jurisdiction, aren't you, fellers?"

Carlton took another big gulp from his glass, wiped his mouth on an already wet sleeve, and said, "That we are, Corky. And we need to talk with your local lawman. Reckon you could send us in the Fort Worth town marshal's direction?"

Smile slowly bled from Tull's beaming countenance, and the gold tooth went into eclipse. "All you gotta do is go back outside. Follow the trolley tracks north. Stay the course for another three quarters of a mile, or so. You'll be able to see the Tarrant County Courthouse at the end of Main, on the bluff overlooin' the Trinity River. Strange-lookin' building. Kinda like the hub of a wagon wheel with some broken spokes still attached."

Nate thumped his mug back onto the bar and said, "Marshal's office in the courthouse?"

Tull flashed another twinkling smile. "Nope. Just gettin' you goin' in the right direction, as it were. When you get to

Second Street, turn right, and go one block to Rusk. City jail and Marshal Sam Farmer's office is on the corner of Second and Rusk, right across from City Hall. Cain't miss it. But should you get lost, and I cain't imagine such an outcome for fellers that made it all the way to the Emerald Saloon from the wilds of Arkansas, just stop and ask anyone. They'll be more than happy to point you in the right direction."

Carlton leaned on his elbows, stroked his beer-dampened chin, and in a conspiratorial tone said, "Get the impression you don't particularly care for Marshal Farmer, Corky. What's the problem?"

Tull didn't miss a beat. "Upstanding citizens of Fort Worth voted him into office over my friend Long Haired Jim Courtright. Now I'll admit ole Jim might've been a bit on the drunken, belligerent side, at times, near the end of his tenure. And he never was able to stop all the stage robberies out west of town. But I always felt safer, on the streets with a proven gunhand running things, than I do now. Besides, them stage robberies is still goin' on."

Nate chuckled and assumed a low-talking stance almost exactly like Carlton's. "Don't appear to be much of a problem for you to voice your opinion on the subject," he offered.

Tull broke into a smile again. "Hell, I ain't afraid of Sam Farmer. Neither's any of the other bartenders, saloon owners, or sportin' men in town. Now if'n I was tryin' to make a living playin' poker, or run a keno game, I might be some worried 'bout the old strong-armed shakedown. That particular legalistic inconvenience tends to come, and go, round these parts. Right now, the marshal's office is on an enforcement-of-all-city-ordinances rip, no matter how obscure. Been hell-on-wheels for businessmen in the Acre for weeks."

"Anything in particular inspire the problem?" I asked.

"City council cut the marshal's salary from sixty dollars a month to fifty. Said he showed no inclination to do his job properly. Caused one cyclonic stir, all over town. Farmer's had a burr under his saddle ever since. If you're going down to talk with the man, be careful. He probably ain't gonna like having outside law enforcement types snoopin' round. Might get to thinkin' as how you were sent for, if you get my drift."

Thumped my empty glass onto the bar. "We'll keep your very astute advice in mind,

Mr. Tull. How much do I owe you for the beer?"

"Nickel a glass. Fifteen cents total."

Pitched him a silver dollar. "Keep the change," I said. "Valuable information and friendly reception are well worth the money."

As we started for the door, Tull called out, "Come again anytime, gents. Been a spell since I rated a tip this size on three glasses of beer."

We got mounted and headed north. Fort Worth bustled with people, wagons, and animals. Main Street was near a hundred feet wide and level, but that's about the only good thing you could say about it. As Carlton noted, the grimy, rutted thoroughfare had the very real potential of turning into a muddy bog with about a teacup of water.

Construction of almost every residential building on either side of the street tended to be from yellow, rough-cut, sap-bleeding pine, and of a type often referred to as shotgun houses back then. Seemed like each and every one of those dwellings had a number of women lounging around outside in various states of dress, undress, and lack of dress.

Half-a-dozen ole gals waved and beckoned us for what I knew had to be a bit of the old slap and tickle. Couple of them even ran over and grabbed at our legs. Heard one hard-looking, brassy blonde tell Carlton, "Git off that damned stinky horse, honey. You can ride me right here in the road fer fifty cents."

Nate shook his head and mumbled, "My sweet Lord Almighty. Ain't this somethin'? Whores is bold in Fort Smith boardin'houses, but ain't nothin' like these."

Larger structures, like saloons, dance halls, and hotels, all sported fancied-up, painted false fronts, and hitch rails. Sizable uncluttered spaces, between the individual businesses and better-known landmarks sought out by travelers, were covered with lumber yards, cotton yards, stockyards, and wagon yards. Lack of cheek-by-jowl clutter found in most towns, and a total absence of anything like a tree, tended to give the entire rambunctious place a definite wide-open, Wild West feel about it.

We moseyed on up the street through swirling clouds of Texas topsoil, past the Headlight Bar, Texas Wagon Yard, City Wagon Yard, and the Mansion Hotel, before coming on a substantial-looking, solid brick inn that took up most of the corner of Third and Main. Place was named the El Paso. Directly across Third Street stood the most famous saloon in Fort Worth. Nate and Carlton looked like a pair of ten-year-old kids turned loose at a county fair with twenty dollars in their pockets and eyes a lot bigger than their stomachs.

Carlton got a toothy grin on his face and said, "Damned if that ain't the White Elephant, boys. I've heard many a story of the place. Folks who've been inside say Luke Short done by-God created the finest gambling establishment west of New Orleans. Reckon we could stop in for a spell, 'fore we head home to Fort Smith, Hayden? Sure wouldn't want to go all the way back to the wilds of uncivilized Arkansas 'thout at least easin' into the premier saloon in all of Texas for a drink."

Nate swept his well-used, Montana-peaked hat off a sweaty head and slapped it against the leg of shotgun chaps. "Hell, yes, Hayden. We gotta stop at the White Elephant, long as we're in town. Cain't go back home and tell our friends we came all this way and didn't see the Elephant."

I waved them into silence. "Ease up, fellers. I'm sure you'll have more than enough time for a drink at Short's world-famous fifty-foot bar before we have to point 'em back to Arkansas again. Don't imagine this dance is gonna be over in a day or two. Figure we'll be in town at least two weeks. Maybe even as much as a month, if things don't go well."

Turned 'em right on Second Street, just past a joint all covered with paper handbills called the Theatre Comique. Sure enough, we found City Hall, and the jail, right where Corky Tull said they'd be.

Tied our animals out front of Marshal Sam Farmer's one-story lockup. Nothing real special about the building, far as I could tell. Appeared to have been recently built. Lumber still smelled, and looked, freshly cut. Other than the heavy iron bars on the windows, the rugged building appeared about like every other board-and-batten shack we'd passed along the way, except it was at least two or three times larger.

Carlton adjusted his weapons as we clomped up onto the boardwalk. "Damn," he muttered, "but I do hate dealin' with belligerent town lawmen. Most of 'em ain't nothin' more'n drunks, thugs, or gunmen themselves. Usually just about smart enough to screw up a two-hearse funeral procession."

Pushed the door open. As Cecil was about to pass me, I clapped him on the back, muttered, "Well, try to behave, Carl. Don't start anything if you can keep from it. Want to maintain as much in the way of goodwill with this man as possible. But if he turns out a problem, we'll just tell him how the cow ate the cabbage, be on our way, and do as we please."

Office, just inside the double-thick door, fronted a cell block that appeared fully capable of holding no fewer than a hundred, maybe more, of the drunk, belligerent, crazy, and unruly. Pair of bored-to-tears-looking city policemen lounged in cane-backed chairs and shoved checkers around on a homemade board, at a table squeezed into one corner.

Oversized oak desk that appeared totally out of place sat right in the middle of the room and dominated everything else there. Deadly variety of weapons filled a gun rack on the wall. A clean-shaven, florid-faced gent in a suit coat, high-collared white shirt, and string tie sat behind the desk and busied himself with a stack of official-looking papers.

He barely glanced up from his scribblings and dismissively snapped, "What the hell you mangy bastards want?"

Can't say as how I liked Farmer's quarrelsome, introductory manner in the least. But I bit my lip, made every effort to remain civil. Went on ahead and explained who we were, as quickly as I could. Presented the surly lawman with our bona fides to prove what I'd said.

Before I could get it out of my mouth why three deputy U.S. marshals from Arkansas had deigned to bother his magisterial greatness, the man assumed a bored-slap-to-tears look, leaned back in a chair that complained bitterly under his abundant bulk, and fired up a fine-looking cheroot. He thumped the match into a spittoon next to the desk, and absentmindedly picked a piece of tobacco off his lip while I talked.

Didn't even manage to get finished when he waved the cigar at me, and set in on us like he'd just found something warm and squishy that stunk on the bottom of his highly polished boot.

"Look, I've got enough problems as it is, *Deputy* U.S. Marshal Tilden. I ain't got time to be a-playin' wet nurse to three stump-jumpin' badge toters from Arkansas. Just what in the hell is it you're here for, anyway?"

Felt like he'd slapped me in the face and left a stinging handprint. Suppose I might have sounded a bit more than peevish when I snapped, "Well, sir, I was about to get to that when you saw fit to so rudely interrupt me."

Farmer's neck colored up a bit this side of purple, so fast I couldn't believe it. About a heartbeat and a half later, his face looked like someone had the man down on the floor strangling the hell out of him. Could tell he wasn't a feller accustomed to being crossed by anyone.

Popped out of his chair like he had coiled-steel springs attached to his butt and growled, "I don't have to put up with no sassy-mouthed road trash from Arkansas shit heels like you, Deputy Marshal Tilden."

Felt Carlton J. Cecil ease up at my elbow. Turned and noticed itchy fingers caressing the butts of his pistols, and that Nate already had the two checker-playing deputies under the gun. My good friend's lips peeled back on his teeth like a hungry wolf about to feed on a downed longhorn steer. Barely heard him when he snarled, "You'd best sit your more-than-arrogant ass back down in that chair and listen to what Hayden has to say, you stupid son of a bitch."

"W-w-w-what'd you say?" Farmer stuttered.

Carl leaned closer. "We're deputy U.S. marshals in possession of warrants issued by Judge Isaac C. Parker of the Western District Court of Arkansas. They're for dangerous men we believe are in your town.

And unless you'd like me to climb over there and kick your ass till that glob of puss you call a nose bleeds, I'd suggest you get to treatin' this man a hell of a lot nicer."

"Why, y-y-you mouthy piece of trail trash," the surprised town marshal sputtered.

Carlton shut him down again when he leaned almost eyeball-to-eyeball with the big tub of guts and whispered, "Wouldn't want to embarrass you in front of your men, Mr. Farmer, but if you don't take a seat, and shut the hell up, I'm gonna whip you like a tied yard dog, in just about two seconds."

The stunned lawman glanced nervously at me, shook his cigar in Carl's face, and said, "You need to put your attack animal on a tight leash, Marshal Tilden. This man's damned dangerous."

Nodded my sympathetic and understanding agreement. Tried mightily to sound diplomatic when I replied, "Yes, he is, sir. An extremely dangerous man. And not one to be trifled with, by any stretch of the imagination. Problem you have is that my good friend here's only about half as bad as me, Mr. Farmer." Unfortunately, it came out cold as ice and menacingly threatening.

Farmer's eyes got the size of saucers as he

stumbled a full step backward and flopped into the safety of his chair. He grabbed his papers and officiously went to shuffling them again.

"Well," he muttered, "guess maybe I might have been a bit hasty, and unprofessional, in my initial attitude, sir. I do apologize. How can the Fort Worth City Police Force be of service to you?"

"You've got a gang of exceedingly dangerous men in your fine city, Marshal. Reports from reliable sources in the Nations lead us to believe that Maynard Dawson, Charlie Storms, and Cotton Rix are hiding somewhere in, or around, your town. Even worse, they could well be in the company of Rufus and Jethro Doome. If such proves the case, you're gonna need our help and, perhaps, that of a company of Texas Rangers to keep brutal murder from becoming an everyday, commonplace event."

Farmer sneered. "I don't think, by God, me or my men will have any problem dealing with a bunch of ignorant, murderin', stump jumpers fresh out of the Nations."

I glanced at Carl. He shrugged as if to say, "What's the use? The man's an idiot on top of bein' a jackass. Let's go find a room, a bath, and something to eat."

Turned back to Farmer. "Well, if these

men kill anyone in your town, you'll know it. Their methods are barbaric in the extreme."

"What the hell does that mean?"

"I'd rather not say right now, Mr. Farmer. Feel it best not to advertise their nefarious and lethal methods. But trust me, sir, won't be any doubt about one of their killings when you see it."

Shook the bigheaded lawman's reluctant hand, and apologized for any misunderstanding. Tried to make it clear we'd work hard to stay out of his way. But let him know, in crystal-clear terms, that we intended on doing our jobs, whatever that might entail. Then, we headed for the street.

Carlton climbed back on his horse and said, "Damn, Hayden, you shoulda let me kick his more-than-stupid ass. Woulda been my pleasure to stomp a bloody ditch in his worthless hide, then stomp it dry."

Tried to calm Carl down as we headed for the El Paso Hotel. Figured I'd spring for all three of us a decent room while we were in town. The El Paso was a splendid and impressive joint. We heard later as how most folks considered it the best hotel in town. Got ourselves a skin-scorching bath and, soon as we could, headed straight for the White Elephant Saloon.

Luke Short's establishment was everything Nate had hoped it'd be. Handbill, posted next to the open door, advertised the bustling saloon and restaurant as open day and night, and proudly boasted of having the finest wines, liquors, and cigars.

I clapped the bug-eyed boy on the back as we strolled past a carpet-covered stairway, leading to the second-floor gambling rooms. Carl couldn't help but laugh at our new partner as we made our way over to the famed solid-mahogany, mirrored-back bar.

"Hot diggity damn," Nate mumbled in amazement, "cut-glass chandeliers. Never seen nothin' like this in Arkansas, Hayden."

Stood my friends to a drink just before a stunning dark-haired, ruby-lipped young woman, dressed like she was on her way to a Chicago opera house, touched my elbow and said, "Would you gentlemen care to dine with us this evening?"

Bold as brass, Carlton snatched his hat off and said, "That we would, miss."

"Well, then, please follow me. You may bring your glasses along, if you'd like." She smiled, turned, motioned us toward the dining area, got us settled, and saw to our every need for the next three hours. That was some of the best money I've ever spent. Worth every penny just to watch Nate and

Carlton try to eat a raw oyster.

After a belly-buster of a meal, we took a brief tour of the gaming area. Joint had a table at the top of the stairs stacked almost a foot deep in gold coins. Have to admit, everything about the White Elephant was damned impressive. Total package put the Emerald, and all those other places down by the train tracks, to head-hanging, dirt-floor shame.

Suppose our stay in Fort Worth might have proved right pleasant had it not been for what happened that first night we were in town, out behind one of Hell's Half Acre's most active and violent dance halls. Repulsive, murderous horror of that bloody night would be whispered about over fences, clotheslines, and behind the cupped hands of decent folk — for years to come.

14
"He Says Somebody Nailed the Poor Girl Up There."

As is the case with all men who spend too much time drinking the night before, the morning after we arrived in Fort Worth came up like thunder before a Kansas cyclone. Dreadful day started before good light with a constant, irritating pounding located somewhere inside my skull, just behind eyes that didn't want to open. Then, Carlton shook me awake.

My bleary-eyed friend swayed beside the bed like a willow tree in a stiff breeze, and scratched at his crotch. Every red hair on his head stood straight out, as though he'd been frightened near to death by something so horrible as to border on the unbelievable. Overall image made him appear as though he'd been shot from a cannon — backward — through a knothole.

He rubbed at his canker-clogged eyes, yawned, and said, "One of Farmer's idiot deputies is at the door. Says their esteemed marshal needs us soon as we can get dressed."

Nate rolled out of the pallet he'd made on the floor and mumbled, "What the hell for? Jesus, what time is it? Sun ain't even up good yet. God, my head hurts."

Carl went to work pulling his pants on. "Idiot deputy says the marshal's got something he urgently wants us to see."

After we'd stumbled into our clothes, and got armed to the teeth, Farmer's tight-lipped, jumpy subordinate introduced himself as Herman Blodgett. He refused to say why we'd been summoned. Led us on a brisk walk to a hellacious rough-looking dance hall, named Smiley's Terpsichorean Delights, located at the corner of Thirteenth and Rusk Streets.

Rank odors of spilled whiskey, vomit, and human waste proved enough for bandanna-covered noses. The constant movement of people and animals around the building had chewed the discarded paper, broken bottles, and littered area fronting the building into a difficult-to-negotiate morass, where at least two unconscious drunks still wallowed about in the muck and mire.

"Marshal's a-waitin' round back," Blodgett said, and pointed along a narrow alleyway between the disreputable building and a crudely erected picket fence.

We waded through more piled-up trash and empty whiskey bottles to a deep, grassless, open area. Situated a bit over midway through the dusty space, between the back door and the fence, stood an enormous four-holer outhouse.

"Jesus," Carl muttered, "you mean to tell me the son of a bitch got us out of our beds, at the crack of dawn, to look at a Fort Worth shit house?"

Farmer, who quietly talked with a knot of other men gathered at one end of the outbuilding, glanced up, spotted us, and hurried over. Man sported heavy bags under his eyes, appeared not have slept since we last saw him. He extended a trembling hand and said, "Glad you and your associates could come, Marshal Tilden. I do appreciate your quick response to my request. Hope you can forgive my inattention yesterday. Had my mind on other matters, at the time. That's no good excuse for poor behavior."

Shook his hand and said, "Quite all right, Marshal Farmer. How can we be of assistance, sir?"

He gently pulled me toward him, placed an overly familiar arm around my shoulders, and guided me to the area where everyone's attention seemed to be focused. "Need you to tell me what you think about this," he said, and turned me toward the farthest side wall of the odiferous building.

Carlton followed and stopped by my side, pulled his hat off, and said, "Good God Almighty. Sure hate to see a sight like this."

Nate almost bumped into Carl. A grunt of disgust involuntarily popped from the boy's lips, as though he'd been struck in the chest by a heavy blow.

Marshal Farmer let his arm drop like a man too tired to hold it up any longer. "Ever come across anything to match such as you see here?" he asked.

The nude, and much-abused, corpse of an obviously young woman hung from the wall. Blond braids, tied to a nail several inches above her head, caused lifeless, open eyes to unnervingly stare right into the stunned face of anyone standing where Farmer had placed us. A sizable, dark, dried puddle of crusted blood, below the poor girl's feet, framed a stack of innards carelessly ripped from her body.

Nate turned away and wiped at a damp brow with his bandanna. "Where's her hands?" he asked, as though to himself. When no one answered, he snatched his hat off, stumbled to a spot next to the dance hall's back door, leaned against the board-and-batten wall, and refused to spend any more time gawking at the despoiled corpse.

Let out a breath that felt like it came from the soles of my feet, then said, "Yeah. We've seen as much, or maybe worse, out in the Nations."

Farmer's chin dropped to his chest. He swayed back and forth like a tired bear. "This is what you were trying to warn me about yesterday, ain't it?"

"Yes. Unfortunately, it is."

"And you've seen worse? Jesus, how much worse can it get?"

Didn't have a chance to answer him that time. Carlton snapped, "Damned right we've seen as much before. And this atrocity just might not have happened if you'd of listened to us yesterday."

Carlton may as well have used an open palm and slapped the distraught marshal's face, right in front of the man's unbelieving wife, all his friends, and employees.

I placed a quieting hand on my angry partner's shoulder. "Wouldn't have mattered what we did, Carl. No one could've prevented this from happening. You know as well as I do, determined murderers can't be stopped. Once they take it in mind to kill someone, we can't prevent it. No one can. Want to blame someone, might as well say it's our fault for not taking care of Dawson and Storms, out in the Nations, when we had the opportunity. Hell, I had two chances myself — failed both times."

Farmer wiped sweaty, still-trembling hands on his pants legs, and talked to the ground. "Doc Fowler acts as our coroner. He says somebody nailed the poor girl up there. Hard to tell from here. Figure it musta took more'n one man to do it, though. Ain't no way a single feller could hold her up, do the nailin' at the same time."

Carl shook his head in disgust. "Anyone know who she was?" he asked.

Farmer waved absently at the corpse. "Deputy of mine says he thinks maybe her name was Molly. Could well occur that we'll never be able to get a complete identification. These girls come and go so much, we ain't got no dependable way to keep track of 'em."

"Sounds like a sad, anonymous way to live," I mumbled.

"Yes, it is. I've already seen more'n a dozen suicides by soiled doves over the past six months. Most depressing part of this job is knowin' young women kill themselves with such frequency. Could be two dozen dead, for all we're able to determine. Sometimes, it's almost impossible to settle on what actually kills 'em. But, more often than not, laudanum usually plays a deadly part."

Carlton shook his head. "Well, shouldn't have no problem figurin' out what caused this 'un. Looks to me like the bastards gutted her, almost took her head off."

"Who found the body?" I asked.

Marshal pointed to a bareheaded feller, who sat on the dance hall's back step, with his head resting in his hands. Appeared as though the poor man might have been crying.

"His name's Winston Pratt. Most folks call him Bug. Don't know why. He works here every night trying to stay ahead of the broken bottles and vomit. Sweeps out, mops the floor, and picks up as much trash as he can every morning. Told me he got here a little earlier than usual today."

Carl scratched his neck and posed the most obvious question of the morning. "You, or any of your boys, really quiz him closely yet?"

Farmer shook his head. "Man's been so upset he could barely talk at all. Cain't say as I blame him much. This killin' has distressed everyone here, this morning. Hell, I thought I'd seen about the worst men could do, but this is one helluva lot worse than the rancher who put his bucket down the well and pulled up a skunk."

Carl signaled me with an almost undetectable motion of his finger. Fort Worth's marshal followed as we strolled over to where Winston Pratt was sitting. Poor boy's head popped up. He shot us a look like a caged rat when Carl touched him on a trembling upper arm. Long, stringy, unwashed hair flipped about on his shoulders as his uneasy glance darted from one of us to the other. Scrawny, and obviously underfed, the panicked boy didn't appear to have yet made it out of his teens. Look in his eyes indicated to me that he was absolutely terrified.

"Swear 'fore Jesus, gents. Ain't had nothing to do with that poor girl's unfortunate ruination," he whimpered. "She was like that when I found her. Never seen a body so badly mistreated in all my born days. Never even heard tell of anything to match it."

Fort Worth's marshal sympathetically patted Pratt's quaking shoulder. "Did you see anyone else this mornin', Bug?"

A look of total confusion quickly spread across Pratt's grit-streaked face. "You mean back here with that poor girl?"

"Anywhere. Out front. Here in back.

Around the girl's body. Did you see anyone else this morning?"

"Pair of drunks in the street, but that ain't unusual. Probably still out there. Weren't no one back here, as I could tell. It were so dark I almost didn't see her myself. Had to drag 'at 'ere barrel over yonder out for haulin' away later today. Gate in the fence is just behind the outhouse, you know."

"When did you first notice her?" Carl asked.

"Walked right up on the body 'fore I realized what it was. Had to bring out a lantern to make sure. Scared me damned near to death when I could really see her. Got chicken flesh on my arms, right this second. Jesus, I still cain't believe she's gone."

Last thing he said lit a spark in me. "Did you know the dead woman?"

"Yes, sir, I most certainly did. She's been working here in the hall, little over a month now. Came from New Orleans. Name was Molly LeBeau — leastways, that's what she claimed. Fancied herself some kind of hightone Frenchified gal. Course her real name coulda been Matilda Smith, or Jones, or Brown for all I know."

Carl rolled a cigarette and handed it to Pratt. As he put fire to it for the still-shaking boy, he said, "Did she have any friends?"

Bug pulled in a lung of smoke and appeared to relax a bit. "Think I heard once as how she had a room over in Lulu Porter's boardin'house, at Tenth and Rusk, on occasion. Worked there, too, you know. Sometimes ran with a razor-carryin' whore named Lucy Love. That Lucy's one more scary female. Cut you up, like a trussed chicken, in a heartbeat."

"Do you think Lucy Love could have done this killing, Bug?" Farmer asked.

"No. Course not. Didn't mean anything like that. Just that I seen her slice up a feller, right here at Smiley's, less than a month ago. Cut a cowboy so bad everyone thought he'd surely pass. Heard many a hair-raisin' tale 'bout that gal. Oh, I can tell you one thing that might be helpful. Both of 'em sometimes worked days at the Two Minnies Saloon, over on Ninth and Calhoun. Might well find Lucy there later this morning."

"And you didn't see anyone else? Maybe you passed someone on the street you didn't recognize on your way to work? Strangers, dressed and armed in a rougher-than-usual fashion?" I asked.

Pratt tilted his head to one side like a puzzled dog. Thumped ashes from his smoke, and suddenly appeared to remember something. He waved the cigarette like a wooden pointer and said, "Well, come to think on it, I wuz makin' my way down the west side of Rusk when I seen three fellers on the east side at about Eighth Street. Couldn't for certain sure identify 'em, though. Way too dark. But I could tell as how two of 'em wuz well over six feet tall and wearing buffalo-skin coats. Curious garb for these parts, considering how hot as it is most days, and nights."

His description sounded familiar, so I pressed him farther. "Either of the men in the skin coats have a severe limp?"

"Yes, by God. One of 'em appeared to have right smart of trouble walkin' at all. Acted like his leg were twisted almost completely around. Maybe clubfooted."

Carlton pulled at my sleeve, leaned close, and whispered, "Bet it's the Doome brothers. Clubfooted one is Jethro. Sure as we're standin' here."

Farmer started to walk away. "Do you mind if we go ahead and do some investigating on our own, Marshal?" I called as he headed for the group of fidgety helpers.

He motioned to his deputies. "Wanna get that poor girl down from there, before we have a crowd gather. Gonna be bad enough when word of this killin' gets around town, as it is. Get a bunch of waggin' tongues and faintin' women gandering at this mess, and we'll never hear the end of it."

Four men stepped forward and began the gruesome task of trying to remove the body. Farmer beckoned me join him, took my elbow, and led me back to Rusk Street. Carlton and Nate followed.

The three of us gathered around Fort Worth's troubled marshal. In a low, conspiratorial voice, he said, "You have my blessings to do whatever it takes to bring the men responsible for this killing to justice, gentlemen. I will instruct my deputies to render any assistance you might need, and will personally inform the county sheriff of my decision and actions."

"Don't worry, Marshal Farmer, we'll find 'em." Carlton sounded considerably more confident that I felt.

Nate nodded his unqualified agreement.

I said, "Do be aware, sir, when we find 'em, we don't intend to take Dawson, Storms, Cotton Rix, or the Doome brothers alive. Far as we're concerned, they're dead already and just don't know it."

For about five seconds, Farmer stared at me like I'd grown another head. Then, he smiled. "Sounds like a damned fine idea to me. Save the county the cost of a trial.

Besides, deputy U.S. marshals, such as yourselves, can rub the Dawson bunch out and head back to Fort Smith with very little in the way of repercussions. But, let's keep this particular piece of information between the four of us. No need for anyone else to share the least familiarity with your plans."

We shook hands all around and, later that morning, Nate, Carlton, and I pushed the batwing doors of the Two Minnies Saloon open and stepped inside. Paused near the open door to let our eyes adjust to the darkness, then eased over to the bar.

"I don't see nothin' all that special 'bout this place," Nate offered.

Friendly whiskey slinger inquired how he could help. Showed him our badges and asked if he could direct us to Miss Lucy Love. He pointed at the ceiling and said, "That's her by the table upstairs. Red-haired gal. Best hope she's in a good mood. Woman can be a handful when she's not." He ran a wet bar rag around in front of us and kept pointing at the ceiling.

Think we all looked up at about the same time. "Just be damned. Now t-t-that's a s-s-sight," Nate stammered.

Carlton turned back to the bartender. "What the hell's it made out of?"

"Four-by-eight sheets of six-inch-thick

reinforced glass."

Nate sounded baffled when he said, "They always go completely bare-assed nekkid like that?"

Bartender offered us a broad, toothy grin. "All day, every day. Cowboys from the massive entirety of Texas know about this place. Just stroll in, order yourself a drink, and a man can see all he could ever want to see for the price of a shot of whiskey. Best damned deal in town. Ain't an ugly, buck-toothed heifer in the bunch."

Less than five feet above our heads, viewed through a glass ceiling, there must have been twenty, or more, totally nude females. Some strutted around, waved, and brazenly exposed themselves in the most lewd manner for anyone willing to take a gander. Others sat at conveniently placed tables and, most astonishing of all, at least half a dozen played tenpins on an alley in the corner farthest from the front door.

"Most cowpunchin' fellers usually end up over yonder, rubberneckin' and watchin' our gals play tenpins. Something they can brag about to their friends, once they get back to the ranch, you see. Course for the right price, man with the money can *have* any of the ladies that take his fancy, out back to one of the cribs for a bit of the ole slap and tickle. You boys interested in a little female companionship of the ride-the-tiger variety?"

"No," I said, "we're here on official business. Would appreciate it if you'd get Miss Love for us. We'll be at that table yonder. Might be helpful if you had her throw something on to cover herself. Don't know 'bout anyone else, but I find it mighty distracting trying to talk to nekkid females."

Carlton flopped into a chair at the table I'd picked, as Nate said, "Would've been a lot more interestin' if'n you'd let her come on down without gettin' dressed, Hayden."

We were still discussing the various merits of having a naked woman at the table, when Miss Lucy Love swaggered up and took the chair between Carl and Nate. "Hear you boys is U.S. marshals or some such. Bartender says you have something you want to talk with me about," she said. Then she dramatically stabbed a smoking cigarette, which had been machine-rolled in blue paper, between lips painted blood red, and waited. Overpowering odors of lilac water, whiskey, and body sweat tinted with a snuffy smell wafted across the table, and almost knocked me out of my chair.

From all observable appearances, Nate and Carl went completely mute, and stupid, when the girl's robe dropped open and exposed most of her pale upper body. She was thinner than my first impression. Couldn't have been much over sixteen or eighteen years old.

"Miss Love, were you acquainted with a young woman named Molly LeBeau who worked at Smiley's dance hall?" I asked.

"Maybe I wuz. Maybe I wuzn't. Whaddya mean 'were'?" she snapped.

"Did you know her?"

She puzzled over her choices for answers a second, and finally said, "Yes. We sometimes roomed together. Still trying to understand what you meant by the question, though. Has something happened to Molly?"

Nate suddenly came back to life. He managed to draw his fascinated gaze away from the girl's exposed breasts long enough to say, "I'm afraid so, Miss Lucy. Someone murdered her last night."

Lucy Love's head dropped to the top of the table with a resounding thump. Both my friends made a grab for her, but it happened too fast. Thought for a second, she'd fainted dead away and possibly knocked herself out, or maybe cracked her skull, when her rock-hard noggin bounced the way it did.

"Jesus H. Christ," she said, and snapped back to a sitting position. Tears streamed down heavily roughed cheeks and smudged the dark liner she used under bloodshot eyes. A quivering hand wiped at the dampness, and further smeared the icing of carelessly applied face paint. "How'd it happen?"

Carl and Nate both shot puzzled looks my direction as if to ask how they were supposed to react. "We can't discuss the details of the crime at this point, Miss Love," I said. "We hoped you could tell us if you saw Molly late last night and, if so, who she might have kept company with."

Lucy Love's pupils narrowed down like pieces of spent birdshot. "There was three of them bastards. Me and Molly'd just come out of Lulu's when they stopped us out on the street. Said they'd be willing to give a handsome sum to whichever one of us'd take 'em all on — at the same time."

Nate leaned toward the girl. Tried to sound understanding when he said, "You weren't keen on the idea?"

She shot him down like a dove hunter using a cannon. "Hell, yes, I wuz willing. Just tired. Been lettin' cowboys ride me all night long. Wuz wore out, sore, and needed some sleep. Ain't no sleepin', if you stay with

Lulu. That woman keeps a warm female busier'n a three-armed bartender at the Local Option Saloon."

Carl tapped her on the arm. "Can you describe those three men?"

"Two of 'em looked like twins. Thought maybe that wuz why they wanted the same girl, at the same time. Tall, nasty, wearing those big ole buffalo coats no one around here wears anymore. Oh, one of them twins had a twisted leg. Limped right smart. Think his friends called him Jethro."

Carl's chin dropped to his chest. "Jesus, save us," he mumbled under his breath.

Knew exactly how he felt. Suspicion was one thing, confirmation a totally different animal altogether. No doubt remained in my mind. The Doome brothers had a part in Molly LeBeau's murder. Only one question remained.

"Can you remember anything helpful about the third man?" I asked.

Girl rubbed a final tear away, wiped it on her thin, almost transparent gown. "Well, it wuz dark out where they stopped us. But even that didn't keep me from bein' able to tell that someone had tried to cut that short bastard's nose off. Had a terrible mess of scars on his face, looked like a map for the Texas and Pacific Railroad tracks."

Nate's glance darted my direction. "Bet everything in my pocket that's Charlie Storms," he said. "Seen him outside McAlester's store one time, several years ago. She's described him near perfect."

Carl touched the well-used girl's arm again. "Did they leave you with any idea of where they were stayin'?"

"No. But if I see 'em again, they'll play hell keepin' me from cuttin' their hearts out. Molly LeBeau might'a been a whore, but she was my friend, a human being, and didn't deserve to be kilt by nobody, for any reason."

Angry red-eyed girl stood, pushed her chair away, and the gown fell open down to her feet. Nate's eyes almost dropped onto the table. She pointed at me, shook her smoking blue cigarette in my face, and said, "You catch 'em, mister. Cause if you don't, and I run across 'em again, there'll sure enough be another killin', or maybe even three."

Barely clothed girl grabbed both sides of her robe, snatched them closed, and stomped away without another word. We watched her trudge back to her lewd duties on the second floor.

"Damn," Nate barely breathed. "Wouldn't want that gal after me." Then he turned to

Carl and said, "Where you reckon she was hidin' the razor we heard about?" Carl grinned, then laughed out loud, and slapped the top of the table.

"Tell you one thing, boys," I said. "Bet this situation is gonna get considerable bloodier before we can stop it. Tell you, Carl, if what we saw out in the Nations is any indication of what to expect, better find the Doome brothers — and Storms — damned fast. Otherwise, Satan's gonna be a mighty busy man in Hell's Half Acre."

15
"Musta Punched a Hole in My Large Gut."

Very night after the discovery of Molly LeBeau's poor battered body, me, Carlton, and Nate spread out in the Acre. Searched every crack, saloon, bar, whorehouse, crib, and cranny available. Talked with all those who were willing to stand still long enough, and carried on with the same dance again — each evening — for an entire week.

Even had some hard-to-ignore handbills printed up, at Carlton's suggestion, and handed one to any working girl who'd take it. But the simple fact always was, when it came to such efforts, you couldn't be everywhere at the same time. After seven fruitless nights on the hunt, our frustration had begun to get the best of us.

Far as I can recall, we didn't turn up a single hint as to where any of the men we sought could have hidden themselves. Experience proved, beyond my ability to understand it, that not one other person we contacted could, or would, admit to having seen Rufus or Jethro Doome, Charlie Storms, Cotton Rix, or Maynard Dawson. Then, with little to go on and nowhere left to look, our most dreaded fears came to pass like an electric bolt of icy-hot death from the blue.

Woke to more frantic banging at our door, on the eighth morning. Deputy Herman Blodgett held his battered hat in his hands and said the words all of us had most feared would surely come. "Sorry to wake you so early again, gents, but we've discovered another body. Marshal Farmer sent me to ask if you might want to come on out and take a look at 'er."

Carlton pulled his shirt over his head. "Well, Herm, don't really *want* to see her, but suppose we'd *better* have a peek. Hadn't we, Hayden?"

With no enthusiasm, I said, "Much as I hate to agree, think you're right, Carl." A sense of apprehensive foreboding, unlike any I'd felt in years, settled over my shoulders like a necklace of anvils.

Blodgett surprised us when he made a kind of deferential, I'm-so-sorry shrug and added, "Gonna need horses this time, boys."

Unexpected pronouncement stopped us all in mid-motion. I stepped a bit closer to our reluctant messenger. “Where’s the girl’s body located, Herman?”

“ ’Bout two miles out, on the Fort Concho stage road. Driver making a return trip found her.”

As he buckled his pistol belt, Nate said, “Man able to see in the dark?”

Deputy sounded a bit shifty with his answer. “Not exactly sure ’bout that, but I know we did have a good moon last night. And some of these stage drivers have mighty fine eyes, you know. Almost a requirement of the job, being as how they spend so much time operating after the sun goes down.”

“This victim treated same way as the other’n?” Carl asked.

“Not exactly. Poor girl’s nailed to a tree right next to the road, if you wanna call that different. Guess the position of the body could explain why the driver spotted her so easy. But there’s something else as well.”

Nate threw his head back and let out an exasperated sigh. “A tree? You did say a tree, didn’t you?”

“Yep. Terrible sight, fellers.” Blodgett gazed at the floor and twisted his hat between nervous fingers. “I thought that last ’un was awful, but, boys, she warn’t nothin’ compared to this ’un.”

“That bad, huh?” I grumbled.

"It's horrible bad, Marshal Tilden. And that's as much I can say right now. Fact is, Mr. Farmer gave me strict orders not to even tell you what I already have. Said he'd have my butt in a sawmill vise, if'n I actually told you what was what."

Figured there was no need to press the agitated deputy any farther. Took us over an hour to get saddled up and make our way to the ghastly scene. By the time of our arrival, the sun had got up pretty good and the searing horror of the grotesque setting fell on us with the full force of an avalanche of stomach-churning revulsion. Charred tree still smoked, and the well-cooked stench of human flesh permeated the air with an unforgettable, sickly-sweet odor.

Nate climbed off his animal, turned away, and refused to look at the body after an initial dose of mind-numbing shock. "What sort of men can do such things, Hayden?" he asked, and whipped his reins against the palm of a trembling, glove-covered hand.

"Jesus, thought I'd seen it all. Probably have nightmares 'bout this till I die. Defies the ability to even imagine, Nate." Hadn't meant to let anything like that slip out, but I did.

With both hands thrust under his pistol belt, Carlton ducked a wagging head, and moaned like a man who'd been shot. "God Almighty, Hayden. Believe this corpse looks a helluva lot more like them we seen out in the Nations than Molly LeBeau did. Leastways, the bastards didn't bother to set fire to poor Molly. This sad girl's condition don't leave one bit of doubt in my mind who done the deed."

Marshal Sam Farmer rushed over, gently grasped my elbow, and pulled me to the far side of the heavily rutted stage road. Poor man looked on the verge of physical and mental collapse.

"Hayden, we've gotta put a stop to these murders, and damned quick," he said. "I kept the story of what really happened with Molly LeBeau to little more than a footnote report in the paper, last time around."

"Would seem to me this killing might be easier to hide for a spell, being as how it happened way the hell out here in the woods, Sam."

He shook his head. "Half-a-dozen devastated stage passengers saw this one, when the coach came on the still-burning body. By now, they're all over town talking their heads off to anyone who'll listen, in spite of my pleas to keep it quiet."

The longer Farmer talked, the more excited he got. Tried to calm him a bit when

I said, "Come on, Sam. Can't be that bad."

Thought the man's eyes would pop right out of his head. "Listen to what I'm sayin', ole son. By the time we get back to town, I'd be willing to bet near panic has set in. Way I've got it figured, if we have just one more of these brutal slaughters, and it goes unsolved, I'll be looking for a new job." Disgusted, he spit and toed at the dirt.

Tried to steer the conversation another direction when I turned back to the smoking tree. "Have any idea who this one is?"

Once more, Farmer shook his head, but didn't look up. "Nope. Not a clue. Very likely we'll never know. Blaze was going pretty good by the time Texas Jack Beck drove the coach from Fort Concho around that curve yonder and found her. He told me the whole tree was afire. Said you could see the flames for miles."

Have to give Fort Worth's marshal his due. Man knew the citizens of his town. By the time we could get that poor woman's crispy corpse down and drag her back to civilization, word of her demise had extended far beyond anything I could have imagined. Rumors, tall tales, outright lies, gossip, and eyewitness reports of every kind, type, and sort imaginable surfaced. As cowboys came and went through town in droves, the story spread out across the entire countryside like the legs of a West Texas tarantula.

For days, the typical street conversation centered on the possibility that bloodthirsty Comanches had escaped the Indian Nations and returned for a final glorious eradication of the invading white devils. After listening to such bilge for almost a week, our luck suddenly, and dramatically, changed for the better.

Had me a comfortable, brocaded chair in the lobby of the hotel, and was reading the latest theory about Molly LeBeau's and Miss X's uncommon murders, when Nate slipped up to my side and tapped me on the shoulder. He leaned over and whispered, "Me and Carlton have one of 'em cornered, Hayden."

Couldn't believe my ears. "Who? Where? How?"

"Carl's got Cotton Rix hemmed up in a room at Lottie Belmont's parlor house down on Eleventh and Rusk. Gotta hurry. Shootin' had already started when I came looking for you."

"You should have stayed with Carl, Nate."

"He wouldn't let me. Said to get you quick as I could. Said the day he couldn't take Cotton Rix, he'd give up his guns, start teachin' Sunday school classes at the nearest Baptist church. Come on, we gotta go. I have my horse. We can ride double."

Nate's powerfully built strawberry roan got us the ten city blocks in record time. Heard muffled pistol fire soon as we turned off Main and hit Rusk. People on the street hid themselves behind anything available. We hit the ground running directly across from Lottie Belmont's place, and headed for the front door of the Red Light Saloon. Had to dodge a pair of dead hay burners, still tied to the hitch rail out front.

Almost ran over one of Farmer's panic-stricken deputies hidden behind the Red Light's batwing doors. Man trembled like he was in the throes of malaria and appeared on the verge of losing his last meal.

"Any more of you boys around?" I asked. Didn't get an answer at first. Had to grab him by the arm and hit him with the same question a second time. "Hey. Pay attention. Are there any more of you city lawmen around?"

He blinked like some of the cogs in his thinker apparatus weren't engaged. "Well, Herman's across the street in Lottie's place. Crazy son of a bitch charged the door, soon as we got here. Too much lead in the air, for my blood."

"Anyone go for Marshal Farmer?"

"I sent a friend of mine, named John Sturgis, to find him. Sure will be glad when he finally shows up. I say let him go over and straighten it all out, by God."

Blasting had quieted down when I said, "Well, if he shows up, he can find me across the street." Slapped Nate on the shoulder. We drew and cocked our pistols, then hoofed it for the wallet-bustin' bordello's front door.

Darted through the gate of a whitewashed picket fence that surrounded the only plot of actual grass I'd seen since we arrived in Fort Worth. Brilliant patch of verdant growth looked so out of place, it caused us both to stumble our way onto the colonnaded porch. The well-kept two-story building stood at the end of a row of one-room cribs that ran all the way around the block. Seemed the perfect place to hunt, if you wanted a whore to kill.

We busted through the half-open doorway — ready to deal bloody death and destruction. A thick cloud of spent black powder smoke swirled around us. Spotted Blodgett under a table beside a polished mahogany stairway leading to the second floor. He crawled out, and scrambled behind us as we sidestepped into the parlor on our right.

"Where's Carlton?" I whispered.

Herman shrugged. "Got me, Marshal Tilden. Somewhere upstairs, I guess. Ain't wanted to try and climb them steps yet. So much shootin' goin' on up there, when I arrived, figured it wasn't a real healthy move. Bet between the two of 'em, they've burned up nigh a hundred rounds."

Nate pulled at my sleeve. "I know where Rix is. He's in the room to the left, at the head of the stairs. Carl spotted him out front at the hitch rail. Gunplay started in the street. Then, we chased him up there. He managed to get the door closed and locked before we could catch him. Went to blastin' soon's he'd slammed 'er in our faces. Gang of screamin' women vacated this place — plenty pronto."

I stepped to the parlor's ornately decorated doorway and yelled up the stairs. "Carl, how is it with you?"

Heard my friend chuckle. Then he yelled back, "I'm fine as frog hair. Don't know about ole Cotton, though. Think I mighta put a dent, maybe two, in his sorry hide."

Muffled voice from a room on the opposite side of the house called out, "Ain't none of you bastards concerned about my health, I guess."

"You hurt, Cotton?" I yelled.

"Damned right, I'm hurt. Carlton J. Cecil

done burned a bad hole in me. Don't think I'm too long for this world. Bleedin' like a stuck hog."

Turned back to Blodgett. Man looked like a rabbit in a coyote's back pocket. "You know of any way for Rix to get out of that room, Herman?"

"Think there's at least one window on his side of the building, but cain't say for sure. Even if there is, he's a good twenty feet up. Only surefire method of departure would involve an ability to sprout wings. If the man's hurt bad as he sounds, be willing to bet he ain't gonna be doin' any flying."

Decided I'd throw caution to the wind and just see how far Rix would go. Yelled, "Wanna give it up, Cotton? You won't leave this place alive if you don't."

"Doubt I'll leave alive anyway. Don't matter none. Always wanted to die in a whorehouse."

In the lengthy silence that followed his weak reply, the settling building creaked, a light breeze rustled the window curtains behind me, and voices from the street got louder. Detected some movement from the outlaw's hidey-hole above and, from God only knows where, powerful odors of lilac and magnolia pushed the acrid smell of fired pistols aside and wafted up my nose.

Got distracted with my sniffing around and almost missed his agonized plea when Cotton weakly called out, "Come on up, you sons of bitches. Ain't in no mood to fight no more, and don't care to die alone."

Herman Blodgett made it plain he'd rather not gamble on the word of an outlaw. Said he'd wait in the little sitting room till we made sure Rix wasn't lying. Can't say as I blamed the man much, but it did reveal a good deal about his lack of willingness when it came to putting his life on the line if the situation at hand called for drastic action.

Nate and me carefully slipped up the stairs and met Carlton as he tiptoed from a room on our right. He nodded, cocked both his pistols, and silently mouthed, "I'll go in first." Man had more sand than the banks of the Mississippi River. Made Fort Worth Deputy Marshal Herman Blodgett look like a belly-slinking snake.

We found the wounded brigand behind a bed in the far corner of the cramped room. Man had a massive hole in his side, about two inches above a blood-soaked waistband. Much of his life had already leaked into a pale pea-green rug beneath his rail-thin body.

He'd wallowed around in the pool of sticky stuff to the point where it had painted his vest, canvas breeches, and cartridge belt. Spent brass littered a bloody lap, and the loading gates of both his .45s lay open. Patchy brown crust covered his face, hands, and the walnut grips of the fancy scroll-engraved weapons.

Too weak to lift either of the revolvers, and barely able to speak, he rubbered his slow-blinking eyes around the room till they landed on Carlton's face. "Think you've went and kilt me, Marshal Cecil." Statement came out slow and painful. "Musta punched a hole in my large gut. Cain't stop this infernal bleedin'. Hurts like Hell's own fire."

Carl leaned over and pitched Cotton's blood-caked hand cannons aside. Said, "Well, you shoulda stopped when I yelled out to you. Instead, you started runnin' and shootin'. Great way to get killed, far as I can see. We've known each other for years, you skinny son of a bitch. Didn't you recognize me?"

Rix moaned. Turned his head away in pain, then said, "Course I knew who you wuz. Knew why you wuz after me, too. Always heard you wuz a dangerous man, Marshal Cecil. Never believed a peckerwood-sized little pissant like you'd be the death of me, though."

I tapped Carl on the shoulder. "Get to the

point. I don't want him dying on us before we can find out what we need to know."

My partner squatted so Rix didn't have to strain to see him. "Where's the Doome brothers, Maynard Dawson, and Charlie Storms, Cotton? We want 'em real bad."

Rix squirmed like we'd somehow staked him to an anthill. "You know how they is, Carl. Them ole boys will kill me deader'n John Wilkes Booth if I tell you that."

Nate shook his head and snorted, "You're probably gonna die anyway, ole son. Best get right with God 'fore you step over the line."

The wounded outlaw's eyes closed for a second. Popped open again when he said, "You boys got any whiskey?"

"I'll send Nate for some soon as you answer Hayden's questions," Carl said.

"You lawdogs won't even give a dyin' man a drink?"

Tried to sound calm when I offered him a deal. "Tell us where Storms and the Doome boys are, and I promise you can have all the whiskey a man can swill down."

"Liquor first, or nothin', Marshal. Ain't got much time left to bargain with you." Rix appeared to collapse inward. His eyes snapped shut. I thought, for certain sure, he'd passed.

Carlton pressed a finger against the bloody man's neck, then smiled. "He's still alive, Hayden. Satan ain't got 'im yet, but the flames of Hell are sure ticklin' his toes."

I turned to Nate. "Go get a bottle. And hurry. He's not long for this world, from the look of him."

"I'll hoof it over to the Red Light. Shouldn't take more'n two minutes."

Swords hustled away. Cotton's eyes flipped open again at the sound of boots clomping down the stairs. "Goin' after my whiskey, is he? Better be, or you boys ain't never gonna get a helpful word out of me."

Carlton jerked the cover off a feather pillow and ripped a towel-sized piece of cloth from it. He dabbed at the open wound, then pressed Rix's bloody hand over the crude bandage.

"Hang on, Cotton," he said. "Won't take him but a few minutes. Have exactly what you want — real soon."

Nate made it back faster than I had any right to expect. Boy took the stairs two at a time, and breathlessly passed the Kentucky sour mash over. I wrapped Rix's obstinate fingers around the amber-colored bottle.

"No glass?" he mumbled. Badly wounded man coughed a gore-soaked laugh out when we all went to rummaging around the room for anything resembling a beaker or a cup. Stream of blood dribbled onto his chin.

"Only kiddin'. Just help me get the bottle up to my mouth. Cain't seem to lift 'er."

Carl helped pour the liquid onto the gut-shot killer's eager lips. Kept it flowing while Rix smacked and slobbered like a kid eating fresh-baked apple pie.

"Damn, that's good," he gasped when Carl backed off. "Things I'm gonna miss most, when I pass, are women and whiskey. Had an unquenchable yen for both since the age of eleven." He lapsed off again and appeared to have fainted.

I pinched a sleeve and shook his arm till he came around. "You got what you wanted, Cotton. Now tell me where the others are."

Thought maybe he'd backslide on me. Buck up and tell us all to go to Hell or something. Given that he'd most likely taken part in the murders himself, such behavior wouldn't have come as any surprise. But luckily, I grossly misjudged the man.

"Cabin. Follow the Jacksboro Road. 'Bout two miles out. Near the West Fork of the Trinity. Cain't miss it."

Tried to reassure him when I said, "You did the right thing."

But, true to his outlaw code, he dismissed

me with: "Please don't tell my pards I done went and give 'em up for a bottle of cheap panther sweat."

Think it surprised all of us some that he turned loose of the information so easily. But his unexpected deed simply went to prove that even thieves and killers can be good for their word, especially if God has an ironclad grip around their hearts and the imps of Hell are rapidly coming into sharp focus.

His blood-scabbed head drooped to one side and clear blue eyes went glassy. Not sure he heard it, but I said, "Wouldn't worry myself, Cotton. If I have my way, they'll all be joining you in the fiery pit soon as we can send 'em that direction."

Carl checked him a final time and shook his head. "He's gone."

Physically drained and mute, we stood and stared blankly at the corpse. 'Bout then, Marshal Farmer and Deputy Blodgett fogged up the stairs with guns drawn like they intended on saving us from a surefire trip to an early grave.

Under his breath, I heard Carlton mutter, "God Almighty, but there ain't nothin' deadlier'n heavily armed men that are so scared they just might shoot each other, or me, by accident." The disgust in his voice came out thick as Red River mud.

Took a bit of doing, but we finally got Fort Worth's brave constabulary calmed down. Managed to move the whole party about halfway down the stairs. Thought all the shouting and turmoil had run its course. Then, Lottie Belmont, lady who owned the place, showed up and the *real* screaming started.

Sturdy woman stood at the foot of her glass-and splinter-littered staircase and wailed like a calf in a south Texas hailstorm. Language that came out of her mouth was enough to make a sailor, who'd been around the Horn ten times, blush.

"Damnation," she screamed at the top of her right sizable lungs. "Look what you crazy sons of bitches did to my beautiful house." She pulled at her short-cropped black hair like someone in torment. "Shot the dog shit out of it's what you've gone and done. How am I ever gonna recover damages on this mess? My God, did you leave anything made of glass in one solid piece? Is there even a single wall you didn't put a bullet hole in? This'll upset the hell out of my girls, Sam."

Farmer tried to shush the moose-sized madam, but she wasn't having any of it. Didn't help his cause much when he blurted out, "Well, Lottie, whatever you do, now, don't go upstairs till we can get the coroner in for a look-see, and then clean the blood and mess up a bit for you."

Color bubbled up the woman's thick neck as she swept Farmer aside like a nuisance fly and lumbered her way to a wailing view of the shot-to-pieces second floor. Harried marshal threw up his hands in resignation and slumped along in the beefy madam's wake. Yelping and bawling sounded like the tortures of the damned. Of a sudden, everything got quiet for about five seconds. Nate, Carlton, and I'd taken up spots near the front door, by then, and I always figured that brief lull in the storm was when Lottie came on Cotton Rix's bled-out corpse.

Motioned my two friends outside and left Farmer to deal with the unhappy madam, the best way he could. We'd barely made the front gate when the shrieking started anew. Could still hear her yelling from across the street at the Red Light. We pushed our way through a boardwalk crowd of the inebriated, inquisitive, and stupid to the crowded bar, and ordered up a double shot of spider killer each.

Took our tumblers of scamper juice and headed for a corner table near the front window. Sat and put our heads together.

Carl got right in my face and whispered, "Gonna let Farmer know what Rix told us?"

"No. What we're gonna do is finish our drinks and vacate this place as quietly as we can. We'll go back to the hotel. Make sure we're loaded for bear, have plenty of ammunition and food, and then we'll head out the Jacksboro Road as inconspicuously as possible."

Nate downed his beaker of fiery liquid and brought the heavy glass back to the table with a resounding thump. Wiped his mouth on his sleeve and said, "Sounds good to me. Let's go gather 'em up."

Carlton grabbed Nate by the sleeve. "Ain't gonna be no gatherin' to it, son. Once we find this bunch, their time on the earth is over. No matter what happens. Even if the whole vicious bunch throws up their hands and begs for mercy, ain't none of 'em coming back to civilization alive. Get my drift?"

The boy turned to me. "Not a problem, far as I'm concerned. But I want to make sure we're all singing from the same page of the hymnal. That how we're gonna work it, Hayden?"

Hit him with an icy stare. "I have no intention of trying to make it all the way back to Fort Smith with such killers in tow. Near as I can guesstimate, here, and in the

Nations, they've murdered almost a dozen people. Half of those unfortunates were women ripped from this life in horrific ways. Carlton's got his saddle on the right horse. We'll find 'em and kill 'em. Kill 'em all."

Couldn't remember a time in my past when I actually looked forward to personally sending a man on his way to whatever awaited in the next world. But Dawson, the Doome brothers, and Charlie Storms lived the lives of men devoid of any feeling or earthly worth, near as I could tell.

The note for Sam Crazy Snake, Hamish Armstrong, Billy Bird, and all those others who'd died in the Dawson gang's gory wake, was past due. I intended on being the man who collected that heart-rending debt. Only currency I felt obligated to accept involved a heavy-duty rendering in blood.

And while there have always been those who would like you to believe that revenge is a sentiment best approached from the coldness of reason, don't believe it. Simply isn't anything more satisfying, in this life, than personally being responsible for sending a heartless murderer on his way to final judgment, and doing it while madder than fiery Hell set loose on earth.

16
". . . Rough Hideaway Erupted in a Thunderous Explosion."

We stopped at Hindershot's Hardware and Farm Implements on our way out of town. Purchased eighteen sticks of dynamite, and all the rifle and shotgun shells we could carry on three horses. Made the feller behind Hindershot's counter right happy.

Headed up the Jacksboro Road exactly the way Cotton told us to go. Turned for the Trinity, two miles out. Split up, spread out, and spent three days searching the heavily wooded bottomlands and bluffs for anything that looked remotely like a cabin.

Got discouraged, and had almost arrived at the point of abandoning the hunt. Nate figured as how ole Cotton might have died like a yellow dog with a blatant falsehood on his lips.

He said, "I'll bet Rix and the devil are laughing about his tall tale right now, while he's cookin' in Hell."

Afternoon of the third day, we found Carlton waiting for us in the middle of an almost invisible wagon road. Leaf-littered path dropped sharply into a tree- and scrub-covered basin atop a steep sandstone cliff, overlooking the river.

Crept up on the rugged remains of a Texas & Pacific Railroad boxcar. A smoking stove-pipe poked through its roof. Rope enclosure at one end of the well-used structure held near a dozen horses. Light breeze blew our direction and heightened the most glaring feature of the place — its odor. Smell could make a man's nose hairs curl up like cork-screws.

"Gamy, ain't it?" Carlton quipped.

Nate rubbed his face and eyes with the back of his hand. "It's a sight more'n gamy. This place stinks like somebody just set fire to a wet buffalo."

We lay on our stomachs on a low rise, about sixty yards away, and scanned the smelly place through Carl's long glass. No discernible activity around the corral. But we could hear loud, angry-sounding voices coming from inside the makeshift hideout.

"How do you reckon a railroad car got way the hell out here in the woods?" Nate wondered aloud, as he handed the glass my direction.

Carl answered for both of us when he said,

"Ain't no real way of tellin'. But from all appearances, she's been sittin' there a spell. Paint's faded and flaked pretty bad, and that appears to be creeping rot over on the end where they're keepin' the horses."

"Sure is ripe, ain't it?" I said.

Carl let out a giggling snort. "Can't imagine what the stink must be like inside for it to be so powerful all the way over here. Smells like a well-used pile of sheepherder's socks. Any luck, maybe the wind'll shift and blow it back toward the river."

Nate rolled onto his back and stared at the tops of the trees. "Had to have been one heckuva job draggin' that thing all the way out here, don't you think? Texas & Pacific's tracks are at least ten miles south. Sure as the devil wouldn't want to try it myself."

Seemed he just couldn't turn loose of the mystery. Got his attention back on the problem at hand when I hissed, "That's Maynard Dawson who just came out the door, boys."

Quickly handed the scope back to Carlton. He snapped it to full length. "Yep, ain't no way to miss a six-and-a-half-foot-tall, one-eyed humpback. That's the man himself, all right. Means the rest of them murderin' skunks shouldn't be far away. With any luck, maybe we've cornered all of 'em in the same hole. Aw, sweet bleedin' Christ, look at that."

Dawson lumbered down a set of wobbly plank stairs and headed across an open area on the opposite end of the boxcar and away from the corral. Man hadn't gone more than a dozen steps when he started jerking at the front of his pants. Stopped about twenty yards from the rugged living quarters and squatted over a barely detectable trench.

Carlton collapsed the spyglass and covered his face with his hat. "Well, that's way too disgustin' for me, fellers," he moaned. "Never did have much inclination for watchin' a fuzzy bear do his business in the woods. Course we could go ahead and shoot him. Mere thought of such an event seems kind of like poetic justice, to me. Be right satisfyin' to watch ole Maynard pitch over into a stinky new and fresh deposit of his own filth."

Nate shook Carl out of his hat. Two more of the drygulchers stumbled into the open air and stretched like waking animals, fresh from a long, cold winter in their dens. Each of them carried his own whiskey bottle.

"You recognize these boys, Marshal Cecil?"

"It's the Doome brothers, Rufus and

Jethro. Suckin' on who-hit-John a mite early — as usual."

"How do you tell 'em apart?" I asked.

"Other than Jethro's clubfooted limp, you can't. Don't know as anyone can. They ain't really twins. Way I heard the story, there's a year, or two, of difference in their ages, but you'd never know it by just lookin' at 'em."

"Well," I said, "now all we lack is for Charlie Storms to show his ugly face, and we can get this dance started."

Barely got the qualifier out of my mouth, when Storms staggered to the doorway. He leaned against the frame and didn't appear inclined to follow his friends to the slit trench for what turned into a group squat.

"Gonna be better if we wait till they're all bunched up together again," Carl said. "Even better still if they go back inside. Then we can surround their foul-smelling nest and shoot it all to pieces with them in it."

Each of us had a rifle, shotgun, three pistols, six sticks of dynamite, and all the ammunition a man could possibly burn up. We patiently waited — and watched — as the objects of Heaven's forthcoming wrath finished their twalet and milled around near the shabby shelter's front door. They smoked, argued, drank, cursed one another, and almost came to blows, at least twice, before angrily stumbling back inside and slamming the door.

"Now's the time, boys. Nate, I want you to stay here. Carl, make your way around back and close off any escape toward the river. I'll move in as close as I can to the front. Don't detect any windows, or other openings. Can't see as how there's any way they'll even know we're in the vicinity till we call 'em out."

"Then what?" Nate wondered aloud.

"We'll wait five minutes for Carl to get settled. Once I've given them a chance to throw down their weapons, count off exactly ten more seconds. Then pour the lead to 'em. No doubt in my mind, they'll fight. This bunch has left too many horrifically abused bodies in their wake. Ain't a one of 'em gonna go easy."

Carl chuckled and snorted, "Sounds good to me." He rolled to his feet and slipped, silently, into the thick stand of oak trees and stunted bushes off to our left.

"Keep your eyes open, Nate. Stay behind this rock over here. Don't want you shootin' me by accident, or getting killed yourself. Carl and I've already lost enough friends chasing this gang of people-crucifying monsters."

As I went into my Comanche tiptoe, he whispered at my back, "Don't worry 'bout me, Hayden. You be careful yourself. See you when this dance is finished."

Rough-cut, chopped, and split logs, piled shoulder high, were stacked less than twenty yards from the front of the bandit den. Figured the Dawson bunch used that jumbled mound of lumber for their cache of firewood. Appeared the perfect place for me to take shelter.

Crept up and scratched a comfortable spot behind the crudely heaped timbers. Laid out everything just the way I wanted on half of a split log. Waved to Nate. Waited till I felt like Carlton had likely built a nest and settled in. Then, I figured it was time to open the ball on those ole boys.

Stood behind my firewood fort with the Winchester propped on my hip and yelled, "Maynard Dawson, Charlie Storm, Rufus and Jethro Doome. This is Hayden Tilden speaking. You men are surrounded by a posse of deputy U.S. marshals. Come out with your hands raised or be prepared to suffer the consequences of your decision."

Barely got the last word out of my mouth when hidden gun ports all along the front of that tarantula's den opened up. Ducked as a flaming barrage of lead blasted my kindling stronghold and sent showers of oak splinters flying in all directions. Sounds, from that bunch of three-tailed skunks laughing like loons, got to my ringing ears, in spite of all the gunfire.

Waited till I felt pretty sure I could hear Carlton peppering those polecats from behind. Let 'em have it with the .45-70. Massive chunks of lead I sent their way sliced through the side of that boxcar like I was cutting warm butter with a hot knife.

In spite of the fact that they outnumbered us, we gave as good as we got for about half an hour. Then, Carlton must have grown a bit impatient and decided to force the issue to some kind of resolution.

Knew something special was coming when all the horses bolted from the makeshift pen. Less than a minute later, that entire end of the rough hideaway erupted in a thunderous explosion.

Blast shook the earth in every direction. Fiery detonation blew at least five linear feet of timber and siding, along with the surprised person of Maynard Dawson, into the shattered air. A hailstorm, of smoke, dust, flame, and splintered wood, fell around my primitive fortress.

Dawson flew end-over-end like a wounded dove for nigh on fifty feet. Landed on his ample rump right in front of my woodpile shelter with his back to me. Stunned, he shook his melon-sized head, rolled to one side, and attempted to stand. I watched, amazed, as he rose on less than cooperative knees, and then actually managed, somehow, to get upright.

Couldn't believe the obviously staggered man had kept from being killed. He swayed in front of me like a tree in a windstorm. Drunkenly, the stunned killer snatched up a pair of pistols, twirled around, and ripped off half-a-dozen wild shots.

Got the groggy outlaw's head lined up in my sights, but before I could drop the hammer on him, Nate Swords nailed the humpbacked scamp four times — dead center. Each separate chunk of lead sent Dawson a staggering step backward and caved his chest in until he appeared on the verge of hugging himself. My new partner's last shot knocked the stumbling murderer onto his back.

Dawson lay still for a second, or so, and then began flopping around. Surprised the hell out of me when he sat up again. The .45-70 slug I delivered to his pea-sized brain finally ended any hope he might have harbored for another day amongst the living. His saddle-thick skull exploded like a blood-filled, rotten egg thrown against the wall of a chicken house. Bullet knocked him flatter than a desert horned toad run over by a stagecoach in Arizona.

Forty-foot flames shot from the blasted portion of the boxcar hidey-hole. Loud popping and crackling noises, amidst the inferno, competed with collapsing timbers, screaming men, and continued gunfire from inside and outside the burning structure.

I was in the process of reloading my rifle, when the Doome brothers stepped onto the wobbly porch. Acted like it was Sunday afternoon and time had come for their weekly stroll to church. Both men carried long-barreled shotguns and brought all four loads to bear in my direction.

Brother on my right yelled, "We're gonna kill the hell out of you, Tilden."

Other one threw his head back and cackled like a madman. "Then we'll nail you to the nearest tree. Set you to fryin' in your own juice. Brag on it for years to come."

Dove for cover as heavy-gauge buckshot splattered everything around me. The woodpile erupted in torrent of splintered chips, dirt, and lead. Heard those big poppers clatter to the ground, along with a flurry of gunfire from Nate's direction.

When one of the Doome boys cried out in

pain, I stood. Figured Nate must have found the range. Spotted Carlton behind a tree off to my right. He'd worked a path all the way around the devastated, smoldering wreck, and pumped shells through a rifle as fast as he could work the lever.

Second Doome boy screamed and grabbed at his side. "Damn, that hurt," he yelped.

"They're killin' us, brother," the first one hollered.

Between the three of us marshals, we riddled the Doomes, and the remaining part of their hideout, with so much concentrated gunfire, you could easily have read the warrants for their arrest through their perforated hides. The bullet-riddled bodies bounced off the wall, flopped like rag dolls.

Dropped my Winchester and grabbed the Greener. As I did, the Doome boys went down on their dead faces like frozen anvils falling in a Montana well.

Moved from behind my cover and took a dozen, or so, steps toward the dead men. Came near making a fatal mistake when I turned to check on Nate and Carlton.

'Bout the time my attention swung back around on those dead outlaws' blazing roost, Charlie Storms charged through the smoke and fire, jumped over the still-fresh, blood-squirting bodies of Rufus and Jethro, and headed straight for me. He had a whiskey bottle corked with flaming rags in each hand.

"You done went and kilt all my friends, you badge-wearin' bastard. Gonna cook you alive," he screamed. Then he pitched one of those crude bombs my direction.

Glowing bottle flew over my head and ruptured in a thump of broken glass and flaming liquid that instantly covered the entire stack of firewood. Strong smell of coal oil attacked my nostrils. Instantaneous heat flashed across my back as the fast-moving blaze ate its way into the stack of dried timber.

All three of us opened up on the crazed killer at the same time. Brought my shotgun around and fired at the hand holding the remaining bomb. Storms attempted to throw the thing at the exact instant I cut loose on him.

Roar from my big blaster, and his left hand instantly vanished in a bloody, vaporous mist. Some of the shot must have hit the bottle. Glass container ruptured in a cascade of sparkling amber slivers. Contents flew all over a stunned Charlie Storms — and ignited. Turned him into a human torch in an eye blink. He screeched like a strangled cat, and staggered my direction.

Carlton joined me as I stepped aside and watched the burning man flail at the flames and fall to the ground, roll around, and throw dirt on himself. Didn't do much good. Canvas coat Storms wore burst into flames as well, and simply made his situation even worse. He pushed himself onto his knees and ripped at the flaming jacket with one burning hand. His hair, eyebrows, pants, even his boots blazed.

Nate strolled up, and we all watched in amazement as ole Charlie the crucifier finally managed to rid himself of the charred coat, and collapsed into a smoldering, stinking heap. Took about another minute for the coal oil to completely burn itself away.

Storms rolled onto his back and let out a pitiable moan. Barely heard the hoarse whisper when he croaked, "Kill me. Please. Put an end to it."

Carlton heard him — plain as day. Stomped over to the crispy bastard's side and shot back, "Man like you don't deserve a quick death, Charlie. Hope it takes a week for you to pass."

Nate pulled at my sleeve. "We can't let him die like this no matter what he did. Hell, Hayden, I wouldn't let a mangy dog go out in such an awful manner."

No doubt about it, the coal-oil bath had reduced Charlie Storms to a might sorry state. Fire had burnt off every hair on his head, and cooked the skin off his face, arms, one remaining hand, chest, and back. Looked like pork cracklin's rolled up all over him. Beneath the layer of seared hide, raw, bloody flesh bubbled and oozed. Even worse, his eyeballs had ruptured. All that liquid had hit his head first and flowed right down to his feet. The heat naturally traveled upward, once it burst into flame, and turned him into a human bonfire.

Pulled my cross-draw pistol and shot Storms between the eyes — twice. Carlton jumped like I'd put a bullet in his head. Nate nodded his approval, then wandered back toward the spot where we'd left our animals.

Carl shook his head. "You are truly somethin', Tilden. Wasn't kiddin' when I said what I did. We should've just rode off. Left him in agony, for as long as it took, till God came to end his sorry life."

Flipped the loading gate open on my pistol and started to reload. "You're right, Carl. That's exactly what we most probably should've done. But I'll tell you, my friend, the feeling I just got from shooting the hell out of him gives me no end of personal satisfaction. Maybe now Billy, Hamish, and all those poor women he killed can rest easier. Think I'll go to my grave with a smile on my face over this one's passing."

We rounded up enough horses to transport all the bodies back to Fort Worth. Drew quite a crowd when we pulled up in front of Sam Farmer's office. He and his deputies stood in the street, flabbergasted at the havoc we'd brought down on the Dawson bunch.

"My Lord," Farmer muttered. "My sweet Lord. You killed 'em all."

"Yes, we certainly did," I replied. "Bad boys put up one blistering gunfight. But they're dead now. As a consequence, you and the good citizens of Fort Worth won't have to worry about finding any more women nailed to trees and burned alive."

Found out there was a sizable pot of money posted on individual members of the gang. Doome boys brought us almost two thousand dollars, by themselves. By the time we added somewhat lesser amounts for Dawson, Storms, and Cotton Rix, the bloody trip to Hell's Half Acre proved right profitable.

Three of us headed back to Arkansas considerable better off, financially, than when we arrived. Nate said he'd never seen that much cash money, in hand, at one time in his entire life.

Soon as we hit the M. K. & T. line, near Sherman, I flagged the Flyer down and sprang for transportation of our horses and ourselves all the way to Checotah. Couldn't wait to get back to Fort Smith and the loving affection of my dear Elizabeth.

Epilogue

So, there you have it, friends. All happened so long ago. Nowadays, I'm condemned to lie here in my bed with General Black Jack Pershing sleeping beside me, so old I can barely feed myself.

But age and deteriorating health hasn't changed my outlook, all that much. I still have passionate feelings about lethal brutes like Charlie Storms. Fact is, my attitudes might have even hardened some over the passing years. Charlie, and anyone like him far as I'm concerned, needed to die. Carlton and me felt it was our duty to accommodate him, and all those others Satan had a soul-stealing interest in.

Today, unfortunately, all the hand-wringers would tear up and blubber about how sad it was that poor ole Charlie's mental illness had taken over and caused him to crucify and set fire to near a dozen innocent souls. Then, they'd set him up in a nice hospital room and see to his aid, comfort, and medical needs till he finally passed on to a just and sulfurous reward. Makes me sick at my stomach just thinking about how gutless society has become when the question of what to do with murderers, thieves, and evil bastards rears its many-tentacled head.

Have to admit, there was one good thing that came out of the Storms business. Got back to Fort Smith and slipped in on Elizabeth at the store. As usual, that beautiful girl had her head in a bookkeeping ledger. Snuck up and kissed her on the ear. She shot out of a leather chair quicker than one of those whiz-bang candle balls on the Fourth of July. Grabbed me like no other man on earth existed. Snuggled into my eager arms and kissed me with such passion my spurs almost melted.

She broke the kiss and said, "Guess what."

"Been gone so long, I can't even imagine, girl. You buy another business of some kind? Have you purchased a meatpacking concern, during my absence? Are we going into the cattle-buying business?"

She tilted her head away from my chest and toyed with my bandanna. "No, silly. Something much more important than any of that."

"Oh, another bank? That's it. You've bought another bank."

Playfully slapped me on the chest. "No, no, no. You made a baby last time you were home, Mr. Tilden. You're going to be a father again. It'll be a boy. I can tell."

Can't recall a time, up till that very moment, that had such a powerful emotional impact on me. Not even the unfortunate deaths of my good friends Harry Tate or Billy Bird. Had looked forward to the day, ever since my son Tommy died. Thought my knees would give way. Elizabeth had to hold me up and help me into her chair.

When she knelt in front of me, I cupped her face in my hands and said, "Would you approve us calling him Billy, Mrs. Tilden?"

A single tear formed at the corner of her eye and carved a sad path down her cheek. Think it matched mine.

"You miss him, don't you?"

"Yes, darlin'. I do miss him, and Harry, too. Could be our way of keepin' their memory alive. Don't you think?"

"Well, then. We'll do it. How would you like a son named William Harry Tilden, called Billy?"

"I think that's an absolutely capital idea."

And so, almost exactly seven months to that very day, a towheaded, chubby-faced, blue-eyed William Harry Tilden came smiling and laughing into the world. He was the joy of my life. And for more years than I care to recall, my beautiful son's presence pushed all memory of Charlie Storms, the Dawson bunch, and what they did, into a closed, seldom-visited corner in the darkest recesses of my mind. I hadn't given those monsters much in the way of thought, until Captain Merchant's ghost came to visit last night.

Gonna close my eyes now. Try to get me some undisturbed sleep. Want to get going early in the morning. Have to beat Leona to the sun porch. Smoke my stinky cigar in peace. Just hope the ghosts will leave me alone.

One night is all I ask, Lord. One night of childlike sleep without a spectral visit. I know. I know. Fat chance.

The employees of Thorndike Press hope you have enjoyed this Large Print book. All our Thorndike and Wheeler Large Print titles are designed for easy reading, and all our books are made to last. Other Thorndike Press Large Print books are available at your library, through selected bookstores, or directly from us.

For information about titles, please call:

(800) 223-1244

or visit our Web site at:

www.gale.com/thorndike
www.gale.com/wheeler

To share your comments, please write:

Publisher
Thorndike Press
295 Kennedy Memorial Drive
Waterville, ME 04901